CANCER

EDITED BY AUSTIN P. SHEEHAN
& HELENA MCAULEY

THE ZODIAC SERIES

The Zodiac Series is a collection of twelve speculative fiction anthologies, each focusing on one of the Zodiac signs. The anthologies feature short stories and poems inspired by each sign, and retellings of the various myths behind those signs.

Capricorn Aquarius Pisces
Aries Taurus Gemini
Cancer Leo Virgo
Libra Scorpio Sagittarius

The Zodiac Series has been produced by Aussie Speculative Fiction, and each anthology contains a diverse selection of tales by talented writers from Australia and New Zealand.

First published by Deadset Press in 2020.

Cover design Copyright © Austin P. Sheehan.

Edited by Austin P. Sheehan and

Helena McAuley.

Foreword by Sasha Hanton.

I AM CANCER

Zoey Xolton

I am the Crab and my constellation is Cancer.

My tarot card is The Chariot; I am an ardent nurturer and am fiercely loyal.

At my best I am tenacious, imaginative and sympathetic

At my worst I am moody, manipulative and suspicious.

Deep and emotional, like my element: Water, mine is a Cardinal sign.

I appreciate art, home-based hobbies, comfort and meals with friends.

However, I dislike strangers, criticism and personal intrusion.

I am ruled by the Moon, and am guardian to the first day of the week.

My colours are silver and white.

About the Author:

Zoey Xolton is an Australian Speculative Fiction writer, primarily of Dark Fantasy, Paranormal Romance, and Horror. Her works have appeared in over one-hundred themed anthologies, with more due for publication!

She has recently celebrated the release of her debut short story collection 'Darkly Ever After'. *You can find further details regarding her many publications on her website:* www.zoeyxolton.com!

CONTENTS:

FOREWORD

Sasha Hanton

The Latin word Cancer means Crab, so it is no wonder that the fourth sign of the zodiac is symbolised by one of these laterigrade crustaceans. This cardinal sign is undisputedly a water sign and, as with the tides, is overseen by the Moon.

Dimmest of the twelve zodiac constellations, the mythology behind Cancer is not terribly enthralling. The most recognised myth of Cancer is a simple one; associated with one of the twelve labours of Heracles (Hercules). During Heracles' fight against the Hydra, the Goddess Hera sent a giant crab to hinder the hero. The crab annoyed Heracles, who killed it, to ensure it would no longer distract him—in some versions he merely kicks the crab . . . all the way into the stars. As a reward for dutifully carrying out its task and sacrificing its life, Hera makes the crab into a constellation. However, because it was not successful in its task she places it into a section of the sky with no bright stars.

Other notable roots of the Cancer sign include: Egypt's representation as a scarab beetle; the Babylonian turtle, or tortoise; and others representing it as a water beetle. Most interesting of all though, is the constellation's title as Gate of Men alongside Capricorn's title of the Gate of Death; the two constellations are each considered a Gate of Gods. In Chaldaean and Platonist philosophy the Gate of Men was considered the gateway through which souls descended from the heavens and took form in human bodies.

As with all signs of the zodiac, Cancer shares a special bond with a card from the Major Arcana of Tarot: The Chariot. Depicted as a princely man holding the wand of authority, in a chariot adorned with a shield and pulled by two sphinxes under a starry canopy, The Chariot is the seventh card in the Major Arcana. Symbolising moving forward at its core, successful conquests when in the upright position and sudden collapses of projects or morals in the reverse, this card is perfectly matched to Cancer's symbolism for new life and fresh starts.

In most versions, the Chariot will be pulled by both a black and a white steed (often sphinxes, but sometimes horses). The black is representative of stern justice and a thick outer shell, while the white is emblematic of mercy and soft inner emotions, alongside the head-to-toe armour the man wears, the card holds a symbolic depiction of a crab—hard exterior, soft insides.

FOREWORD

Maternal, domestic, and loving are the traits most frequently assigned to individuals of this star sign, along with a good memory and a tendency to retreat into themselves (much like their symbol the crab). Born to wear their hearts on their sleeves, Cancerians tend to be emotional and can be impossibly hard to get to open up when they don't want to. And whilst their ruling planet is no planet at all, but rather the Moon, it is a fitting appointment as their moods appear to turn as quick as the tides.

Every general aspect of Cancers can be traced back to their symbol, the Crab, or their ruler the Moon. While the Moon isn't a planet, or named for a god, there are multiple mythic goddesses associated with it which is perhaps why it is associated with motherhood and fertility. Those born between June 21st and July 22nd will find their sun sign makes its home in Cancer.

Cancer individuals can be highly creative, protective of their families, and well suited to team sports: among other things. While on the surface it may seem simple to derive what the sign Cancer is all about, as you read through this anthology you'll find there is much more to the Crab once you get beneath its shell.

About the Author:

Sasha Hanton grew up in the tropics of Darwin, Northern Territory. From a young age, she devoured books and iced coffee, both of which she continues to intake on an almost daily basis. Now living on beautiful Bribie Island in Queensland, her time is split between writing and spoiling her puppy Miley.

Sasha, who has a Bachelor of Journalism from Bond University, has dabbled in the journalistic profession but finds fiction far more fascinating. Her first published work The Short Story Press Collection *draws on her love for a diverse range of genres and passion for short stories. Coming from a multicultural background (Eurasian) she aspires to make her writing inclusive for people from all walks of life and to bring a unique blend of eastern and western culture to her writing.*

Throughout her life, she has been a lover of history and mythology, and at any time will find some way to worm one or the other into her storytelling. When she's not writing or reading she can be found walking her dog and volunteering. You can keep up with her writing over on www.theshortstorypress.wordpress.com

4

STASIS

Eva Leppard

Emily tilted her face back, closing her eyes and letting the chilled fingers of wind graze over her exposed skin. The grey-to-black sky loomed so low she felt she could almost touch it, and that— coupled with the glassy oil slick sea that her boat skittered along— gave her a feeling of safety, almost security.

She had a pretty low bar for feeling 'safe' at the moment, apparently. Her standards were diminishing by the day.

That might be the whole point, come to think of it.

Her hands grasped the sides of the roughly fashioned coracle, and she peered down into the thick, dark water. Impenetrably black. There could be a massive creature directly below her and she would have no idea, until . . .

She shook the thought from her head and rebalanced her weight on the small seat. With no oar, no way of propulsion, she was at the mercy of the currents and the eddies that swirled around her, visible one moment, gone the next. Seemingly moved by an unseen force.

Darts of rain had begun to fall, although with the strong wind and the heaviness of the clouds, they came at her horizontally. Well why not? She may as well get wet now, too. She was cold, lost and overwhelmed by the enormity of what was happening. The icing of a very very ordinary, probably sugar-free, cake.

A soundless vibrating tone echoed over the water. It came from the very atoms from the air; from the water itself and from the sky. It swelled until every molecule in her body rang in a song that responded to the tone, a primordial, timeless Ohm that filled her head, the world, and every drop of water in the endless ocean she sat so delicately upon. Emily tried to cover her ears but it didn't help. The soundless sound was in her, it was in her and it was in the very fabric of time and nothing could stop its call that rang out through the eons.

It stopped.

It stopped as suddenly as if someone had thrown a switch. It didn't just gradually fade, as the echoes of an enormous bell would fade; it cut off as if the sound had been sucked from the air.

Everything was still. The rain and wind had stopped. The water had ceased its endless twirling and twisting; the paths of currents that stretched off all around her had smoothed out. The sea was a glassy black mirror, reflecting the sky that seemed ever lower now, if that was at all possible.

Actually . . . She peered up into the sky, so seamlessly covered with clouds that it was hard to see where they stopped and the horizon began. Were they closer?

They seemed to be closer.

Goddammit.

She raised her hand, trying to judge the distance above her. It was almost impossible to know what she was looking at, like she was looking into an optical illusion. She reached her hand up even further, wary of standing on her tiptoes on the unsteady surface. Adjusting her weight, she raised herself slightly, and . . .

Touched the sky.

She touched the sky. Not in a metaphorical, euphoric sense; but literally. Her hands touched a damp solidity. Emily pressed them up further, and her fingers were engulfed by something that could almost be marshmallow. So viscous and sticky and thick that when she jerked her hand back towards her, there was a palpable feeling of sucking, as if air was rushing in to fill the space that her hands had made in the sky.

Jesus. She stared at her hands. A white sticky substance coated them, then dissolved, leaving a faint stinging sensation and the beginnings of a red rash that pricked her skin.

It was moving down towards her, bubbling and boiling as it moved down ever closer to her head. The thought of that thick mass touching her face, swarming over her head, her hair, her skin. The sky was reaching out to her, undulating and swarming.

sound like rustling paper came from the very heart of it, the noise of sentience, the noise of a creeping sentient, yet mindless, desire.

The decision made itself.

She jumped.

Thick.

Warm.

Like blood.

Sinking into the blackness of the ocean, she tried to kick her legs, but the viscous mass held her, caressing her as she forced her way to the surface. As Emily forced her head above the surface, the gasped in a lungful of air, a sweet salty taste in her mouth.

She barely had to move to keep herself upright, the liquid cocoon gave her a slight buoyancy and her body relaxed into the pulsating warmth surrounding it. Lifting her hands to her face, the blackness ran slowly down her hands and arms, sinking back into the depths.

Above her, the clouds seemed to be retreating; or at least they were not sinking down any further. They hung higher now, she was sure of it. Just out of reach, the coracle meandered away, caught in another one of the inexplicable eddies that had brought her this far.

The noise began again.

The pulsating, undulating Ohm that had filled the world was coming from beneath her. It echoed up from the depths, the pulsating waves increasing in intensity as they moved up, through her, through the sea, into the empty space, the sky. She realised, that the vibration and the sea and the clouds and the air were communicating, were sharing, were speaking into reality the fact that she was there, and they were aware of her.

Something was coming.

Beneath her, she could feel something was coming.

Something huge was pushing up from the depths, changing the very substance of the liquid around her.

It crested the surface about a hundred metres away, a brown monolith bursting from the sea, liquid pooling off it like oil. It grew, its massive shape rising and rising, until a gargantuan crustacean loomed above her. With a growing horror she realised that this was it, this was the thing that she had to confront. Until she did, she would never have the strength to take on what she . . .

A small door opened in the sky above her, and a fierce beam of light spotlighted her in its glaring glow.

"Are you right down there?"

Emily paused to wipe the liquid off her lips. "Yeah fine thanks."

"It's just that I thought I heard you yelling."

"No, no yelling. Not from me anyway. Check the biome next door."

"No they finished a while ago. It might have been the Biome of Infinite Boredom then."

"Ok."

The light continued to blind her.

"Time's up anyway, love. Head up when you've got yourself organised."

A thick rope, ribbed with chunky, graspable knots was lowered from the door, and Emily grasped it, hanging on while it lifted her up and out of the world. She grabbed the edge of the doorway and lifted herself over, falling onto the floor of a stark, white room. A woman in a sensible head wrap and an apron held out a towel. She wore a name tag that stated, plainly, 'Trainer.'

"The hot water is on the blink sorry. Are you right with a cold shower?"

"Not really."

The woman stepped back and regarded Emily. The thick water pooling around her feet, her hair was plastered across her face. "If you try to put your normal clothes on now you'll make an absolute mess of them."

Emily took the towel and headed to the shower. "I didn't say I wasn't going to have one, I just said I'd rather not have a cold one."

"How was it down there?" The Trainer mopped up the water stagnating on the floor, and pulled down several levers attached to a wall. The door had disappeared, sealing itself back into the alter reality where the sea, and the monolithic crab, and the skies, existed.

The fact that the world existed, somewhere, was deeply unsettling to Emily, as freezing water washed the alien world's detritus from her, but 'deeply unsettling' was the whole point of this, after all.

The trainer held Emily's clothes out for her as she stepped from the cold shower.

"You did well. The assessors just radioed through. They liked the way that you coped with your imminent demise, what with the toxic sky falling and all. I mean, putting your hand into unpleasant substances may seem a bit gauche and predictable but you'd be surprised how often it will happen to you. You need to develop an almost nonchalant attitude to it. And you didn't burst into tears when the Prophetic Ohm began, so there's points in your favour."

"That Prophetic Ohm is the worst bit. It gets right into your head. I felt like I couldn't escape. I was trapped with this huge noise and I just couldn't get away." Emily shuddered involuntarily.

"Yes, that's right. Can you tell me how that will apply in your future situation?"

The Trainer asked the question lightly, but Emily knew that her words were being recorded.

"I suppose that it's about the noise. The noise that seems mindless but actually has a deep consciousness to it. It gets into your very soul but you can't do anything about it. I suppose that's something that I need to get used to."

"Oh no love, you never get used to it. But you learn to cope with it. You develop your own coping mechanisms so, when it happens in your future situation, you won't run screaming. You did well."

"How about The Beast?" asked the Trainer as she helped Emily rub her hair dry. "Did that bring about a kind of deep existential angst in you? It's meant to create a kind of ancestral dread. A kind of a deep, visceral fear for your own life and even for the future existence of the entire human race. Seeing that may well make you doubt whether we can keep going as a species."

Emily buttoned her cardigan. "I suppose that its application to my future career then, is that no matter now scared I feel, no matter how threatened, no matter—"

"No," the Trainer interrupted her. "No, it's just meant to scare you. No lesson there. Just scare you shitless, basically."

"Oh well, mission accomplished then."

"Look, I shouldn't say anything to you, but—" the woman leaned forward conspiratorially. "But the student in the other biome tapped out."

Emily looked at her in shock. "What, the Tactile Biome? The sentient jungle? With those little animals that follow you around hugging your legs?"

"Yes, he just couldn't handle it. He couldn't handle being 'got at all the time,' as he described it. So you're another one down. This is looking good for you."

Emily shook her head in disbelief. "That was the easiest biome that I've completed."

The Trainer shrugged. "Well, different people can handle different things. The Tactile Biome breaks some people, but you flew through it."

Emily ticked off a list on her fingers. "I've done the Tactile Biome, the Prophetic Ohm Biome, the Biome of Infinite Boredom, and the Biome of Passive Aggressive Colleagues."

"That one was hard for you," reminded the Trainer.

"Yeah, talking of breaking people. That one was the worst."

"Yes. These are all the kind of things that you will have to be dealing with."

"And now I have to go and write essays on them all."

They exited through the white, modular door together, the Trainer flicking off the lights as they left. "You'll be fine," she said. "I have great confidence that you'll make it through with flying colours. I have a good feeling about you, and in twenty years of doing this job I've never been wrong."

Emily smiled. That made her feel a bit more confident.

"Of course, nothing that we can do here can really get you ready for what you will have to endure. We can't replicate it exactly, but we can do our best with the theoretical lessons, the personality tests and the Reality Biomes. But even if you get through it all—"

"I know," finished Emily. "We're on our own. Once we take on this job, and shut the door every morning, we're on our own."

The Trainer turned and hugged her, forgetting decorum for a moment. "I know that you can do it."

They parted ways at the front door, Emily slinging her backpack over her shoulder and heading down the worn footpath.

The Trainer smiled after her. She hoped that she made it, she really did. She had developed quite a soft spot for Emily. She sometimes wondered if she should discourage those ones, the ones that she really liked. It was a hard life. But, she sighed, flicking the last of the lights off as she locked the door behind her; it's their choice. They know what they are getting themselves into after all.

Above her, the bright sign that emblazoned the front of the building went dark, and the illuminated words; 'Kindergarten Teacher Training Academy' blinked out for another day.

About the Author:

Eva Leppard lives in the bush with her husband, children and a disturbingly large number of rescue animals, many of who she raised by hand whether they liked it or not. For someone who claims never to have enough time to get everything done, she subscribes to a lot of streaming services.

Of the Sea, Stronger Together

Stephen Herczeg

Jed Crùbag strained to turn the winch on his crane. The groans coming from the crane as it slowly dragged the crab cage to the surface told Jed he had a great haul. The season had been good, and the weight of the cage confirmed it. Finally, it broke the surface and Jed could see the writhing mass of blue shells inside. He pulled, struggling at the bulk and almost dropped the cage when it caught on the edge of the hull.

I'm getting too old for this crap.

He caught his breath and wiped his brow.

But you can't afford another fellar, so get on with it.

As he managed to heave the bulky iron trap on board, he peered in at the dozens of shiny black eyes staring back in fear and hatred. Dozens of tiny claws clicked their distress and anger.

Jed looked at them for a moment and smiled. "You'll bring a pretty penny at market tomorrow, I can tell you that," he said to the mass of crustaceans straining at the thick wire of the pot.

The crabs were his life. He'd keep some for food, the rest he'd take down to the nearby seafood market. One good trip like today and he could live off the proceeds for weeks. The city slickers liked nothing more than fresh deep-sea crab or lobster. As for himself, he didn't need much nowadays, and the half dozen pots full of crabs he'd managed to bring up would see him through for a while.

One more trip like this and I'll be set for winter, I reckon.

He emptied the crabs into the large water filled bin sunk beneath the middle of the deck. They joined the rest of their kin that had come aboard earlier.

Jed looked down at the mass of crustaceans and sized up the total load. Satisfied, he stacked the empty pots and secured them for the journey home.

Time to give thanks.

Jed raised the hook on the aft crane. Back at home, he'd use this crane to offload the crabs, but it was his family's custom to pay the denizens of the sea a small token of his appreciation.

Attached to the hook was half a beef carcass, dressed and ready for consumption, but not by Jed or any other human. This was for the fish, crabs and anything else lurking below. The Crùbags had been fishermen for their entire history. Originally from Scotland, now all but gone, except for the remaining member of the clan whose home was on the south coast of New South Wales.

Jed swung the carcass out over the water and cut the rope holding it in place. The offering splashed into the darkening sea and floated for a while, attracting all manner of small fish to investigate, before sinking down into the depths to feed the next generation of crabs.

"Don mhuir bheir mi taing."–To the sea I give thanks. Jed watched the carcass sink out of sight, then turned and picked up one more offering from its secure hiding place beneath a nearby bulkhead.

As Jed stared at the bottle of whisky for a moment, a small tear formed at the corner of his eye. He wiped it away then tossed the bottle from the boat. It plonked into the water and bobbed back to the surface.

Jed watched the bottle bobble about on the surface, as ripples fanned out around it. Ever since his son had become a man, they had shared a bottle on each of his birthdays. Since the seas took him two years ago, Jed had never felt so alone in the world as he did at that moment.

"I miss you boy. I know you can't have a drink with me anymore, but I still want you to know I think about you every day and especially on your birthday," he said staring at the bottle.

17

Tears began to flow. He wiped them away with his sleeve before turning away and heading into the cabin. The motor fired up and Jed's trawler moved away from the crab grounds, leaving the bottle floating on the empty sea.

When Jed's boat was well out of sight, the bottle quickly sank into the depths as if snatched from below.

With his boat, the *Niamh*, securely moored to his small wooden dock, Jed walked up to his little shack. The sun had gone down for the day and a bright moon shone over the little inlet that Jed called home. Small ripples washed into the bay and broke gently on the shore of golden sand that bordered the land.

As Jed stepped onto the porch of his little wooden cottage and put his hand on the doorknob, his eyes were drawn to the small carving above the doorway of a blue shield with a white cross running diagonally across it. In the bottom part a golden crab sat with its claws raised. Two gold fleur-de-lys sat in the triangles to the side of the cross. In a scroll above the shield Jed's surname, Crùbag, was emblazoned. In a scroll at the base were the Gaelic words, *'Den mhuir, làidir còmhla'.*

"Of the sea, stronger together," he muttered under his breath. As he stared at the word *together* for a moment, another wave of utter loneliness washed over him. He took a deep breath and gathered himself before opening for the door.

Jed pushed the unlocked door open, made his way to the kitchen and plonked the string bag filled with struggling crabs in

18

the sink. "You lot should be a nice supper, I tell ya. Can't get much fresher, I reckon."

He stepped over to the deep brick fireplace that served both for cooking and heating. Within a few minutes he had the fire started with a large saucepan full of water hanging above it.

Jed enjoyed the warmth as it bled through him, erasing the cold chill in his bones from a day on the open sea. He stepped over to a nearby cupboard and poured himself a glass of whisky. The small photograph of a young man sitting on the mantlepiece stared back at Jed as he moved back to the fireplace. He smiled at the image which could have been him in his twenties and tapped his forehead with the glass, saluting the photo, and said, *"Slàinte. A mhic, bidh mi gad ionndrainn gu bràth."*—Cheers. My son, I'll always miss you.

He downed the fiery liquid in one gulp, his eyes misting with tears. "That's the closest I'll get to sharing a drink with you today, unless you manage to open the bottle, I left you."

The pail of water sitting above the fire began hissing and spitting as the bubbling water hit the flames. Quickly moving to the sink, Jed grabbed a pair of crabs from the bag. Careful to avoid their snapping claws, he brought them back to the fireplace and dropped them into the boiling water.

The little crustaceans squealed as they hit the water. Jed returned to the sink, grabbing the last two and dropping them in with their mates. His stomach gurgled in anticipation.

"'S gonna be a nice dinner."

19

It was early the next morning when Jed noticed the buff coloured envelope lying on the floor near his front door. He picked it up and eyed it suspiciously. His full name and address had been printed on the front, but there was no stamp or return address.

He sat down at the table and sipped from a mug of hot, black coffee as he opened the envelope. It contained a letter printed on expensive paper, the sender's name and address were alien to Jed.

The letter read:

Dear Mr. Jedediah Crùbag,

First let me introduce myself, I am Douglas Kirchebner of Kirchebner Developments. My company develops seaside resorts and hotels all across this great nation of ours. We are interested in developing a new family-based resort and Suffolk Inlet has proven to be the ideal location.

I would like to offer you two million dollars for your family's land holdings and can also assist in your relocation expenses or the purchase of a residential unit in the resort.

I will be travelling to Bradbury on the twelfth of August and would relish the opportunity to talk to you about the mutual advantages of this offer.

I urge you to strongly consider this offer. I hope we can come to an advantageous agreement when we meet on the twelfth.

The rest of the letter suggested Jed contact the company's office and arrange a suitable time. In his mind, Jed simply read, "blah, blah, blah." He had never considered selling up or moving on. He would die on this land, like his father and his father's father before him. It was Crùbag land; had been since the first fleet had landed and disgorged its contents of prisoners onto the wide brown land of Australia.

Jed read the letter once more, harrumphed, screwed it into a tight ball and threw it at the fireplace. It bounced into the dwindling pile of red coals and burst into flames, lending a brightness to the dull morning for a moment as it flared.

Turning back to sip at his coffee, he said, "City folk. All the same, wanting to make the wild lands like the city." He chuckled. "Good luck with that."

Jed sat on his chair down by the dock repairing several small dents and cuts to the crab pots.

"Little beggars," he muttered "You'll never get out of these cages, but you damn have to try and ruin them."

A bright glare of sunlight played across his eyes. A long black car pulled up on the hill overlooking the inlet. The doors opened and four men stepped out.

At least he didn't try to drive down here. Last idiot to try that ended up in the drink.

Two men, dressed identically in dark suits and sunglasses, stood by the car while the others crunched their way down the gravel path towards the dock.

The older one was bald, with the stretched skin of someone who had relied on surgery to keep their appearance young. Jed

21

had read about such idiots in some of the magazines at the doctor's surgery when he went for his yearly check-up. The other looked like a before image of the older. He had a full head of hair and more of a confident gait as he made his way down the path.

The men reached the dock and the older one stepped forward with his hand outstretched. "Mr. Crùbag, I'm Douglas Kirchebner."

Jed's face dropped; a slight sneer came to his lips. "Ah, bugger, is today the twelfth? I thought that was tomorrow. I shoulda been out on the water today, just to avoid you."

Jed watched the other man's hand drop away and his face grow stern.

"You read my letter then," Kirchebner said.

Jed eyed him up and down, not hiding his animosity. "I ain't selling and nothing you can say will convince me otherwise. This is my land, has been my family's land for generations. Since the first fleet in fact. When I die, I'll be buried here, like my ancestors." He nodded toward the small graveyard on the neighbouring hill.

Douglas smiled. "Admirable," he said, "I completely understand your connection to this land. That's why I made the offer that I did. Two million dollars and your choice of villas in the new resort. With that, you could live out your days in luxury." He turned towards the cottage. "A vast improvement on your current arrangements."

Jed followed his gaze. Even though his cottage was basic, it was his home, had always been his home, and he wasn't going to have some tarted up city boy coming around here and putting it down. "Don't deal with country folk too often, do ya?" Jed fired back.

Kirchebner held up his hands defensively. "No, sorry, I didn't mean anything malicious. All I meant was that you would have all the creature comforts you could want and a lot of money to live out the rest of your days in style."

"Yeah, nuh. I'm fine just where I am," Jed said.

Douglas eyed the older man for a few moments, then put his hand inside his jacket and withdrew a folded piece of paper. "I'd like you to have another think about it, Mr. Crùbag," he said.

"This is a contract between you and I. Man to man." He passed the page to Jed who cast his eyes across the printed words. They seemed to say the same as the letter he'd received.

Kirchebner reached into his right jacket pocket and took out a cheque-book. He flipped open the book and started to scribble on the cheques inside. He tore two off and handed both to Jed. "That one is for a hundred thousand dollars. I've signed it in good faith. That's for you just to have another think about my offer. Even if we don't come to an agreement, you can bank that one. The second is for four million dollars. I haven't signed that one. When you are ready, call my office and I will return within a couple of hours and put my name to it. If you don't mind, I'll come back in two weeks regardless and we can chat again."

Jed looked at the printed page and the two cheques. His expression remained impassive. He knew that this idiot wasn't going to leave until he agreed to think about things. "Alrighty then,

I'll give it some more thought. I don't think that anything you've said's gonna change my mind, but . . ." He shrugged.

Douglas smiled and nodded. "That's all I can ask. I'll see you in a couple of weeks."

Jed watched them head back up the gravel pathway. The son stared at Jed for a moment before joining his father. Picking up the cheques, Jed read them and simply shrugged before putting them to one side and placing a pair of pliers on top to stop them blowing away.

The two dark suited men standing near the car had their gaze zeroed in on Jed while the Kirchebners climbed the gravel path.

"What's he been doing?" Douglas asked as he approached.

Les, a mountain of a man, said, "He read the letter then put it aside."

"That's something I suppose. He could have just screwed it up," Douglas said.

"He's not going to sell," said Terrence, Douglas' son.

Douglas turned and peered at the old man as he went about fixing his crab pots. "Yeah, you're right." Douglas scanned the area around Suffolk Inlet, the vastness of the ocean sent a shiver through his insides. Douglas knew a great location when he saw one but was more than happy to stay well away from the water. "This place is too good to pass up. I want it. The resort I'll build here will be the best in the state. I don't want any brain-dead fisherman ruining my plans." He turned towards Les and tapped him on his chest. "Keep an eye on him. Give him a couple of days. If I haven't heard from him by then, you know what to do."

Jed rinsed out his coffee cup and put it in the dish drainer. He stared out the window at the lightening sky. After three days of horrible weather, the sun was just peeking over the eastern horizon, bathing the scattered clouds a brilliant yellow.

Nice day for a fish.

He turned away from the sink. His back groaned with pain, a reminder of just how old he was getting. He shook away any thoughts of staying ashore.

Last trip before winter, so time to get out there amongst it.

As he stepped towards the door, he noticed Kirchebner's letter and the two cheques. He reached over, picked them up, and read the letter again. A tiny spark of favourable thought appeared in the deepest recesses of his mind. Jed stared at the hundred-thousand-dollar cheque. It was his, after all. He could last years on that alone.

Well, I had a think, that was all the man asked me to do.

He looked again at the unsigned cheque.

Four million dollars.

Jed didn't even know what to do with four million dollars. He dropped the cheque back on the table and noticed his son's photo on the mantle-piece. That made his mind up.

This place is all I've got to remember you by. Stuff it, I'm staying.

Jed put the contract and unsigned cheque into the fire. They flamed up quickly and disappeared. He looked at the hundred-thousand-dollar cheque in his hand.

I'm keeping this one though. I'll bank it tomorrow. Man's got to plan for the future.

Placing the cheque on the table, Jed plonked a saltshaker down on top to keep it in place. As he stepped outside, he spied the magnificent sky, bright with sunshine and a sea as smooth as glass.

This is gonna be a wonderful day.

Puffing from the exertion of bringing the last crab pot aboard, Jed stood leaning over the side rail of his boat and dragged air into his lungs. He put his hands on the small of his back and cringed at the crackles and pops from his spine as he leaned back.

Crikey.

Dumping the last of the crabs into the hold, he stacked the pots and peeked at the sun dipping low on the western horizon. He didn't want to be out here for too long in the dark, it always made the last part of the trip a little more dangerous.

The drone of another boat caught his attention and he spied a small trawler heading his way.

Strange. Why would they be coming out at this time of the day?

By the time he'd tied everything down and started the motor, the other boat was almost on him. He waved a greeting but was met with a steely gaze from the pilot of the other vessel. Shrugging, he pushed the throttle forward and the motor roared to life. As the *Niamh* pulled away, the other boat turned to starboard and cut across his bow. Jed cut the power, but momentum took the *Niamh* forward and she slammed into the side of the other craft.

"What the hell?" he shouted.

A dark suited man appeared on deck and threw a rope over one of the Niamh's cleats. He drew back on the rope and wound it around a cleat on his own boat. Jed came out of his cabin and climbed onto the starboard railing. As he edged his way along until he stood on the bow housing, he yelled, "What in hell do you think you're doing?"

The other man's gaze was intense behind his expensive pair of sunglasses, filling Jed with fear. As the man pulled out a small pistol and aimed it at Jed, the old man's hands raised automatically. "I ain't got nothing but crabs. You can have 'em all."

"I don't want your crabs, you stupid old git." The man reached into his other pocket and pulled out a folded sheet of buff coloured paper. "I want something far more valuable." The dark suited man stepped across onto Jed's boat and motioned with his gun towards the stern. "Andy," he yelled over his shoulder.

Another young man in his late twenties appeared on deck. He was dressed similarly in a dark suit and it finally dawned on Jed who these two were. He'd seen them a couple of days ago, standing in front of Kirchebner's dark car.

27

Damn. That bastard's double crossed me.

Jed hurried along the railing and stepped down onto the deck of his boat. He searched around for a weapon but stood up straight when he felt Les' gun barrel press into his neck.

"I was about to sign the contract and call Mr. Kirchebner, I just needed to make this trip before the storm season hits," he said standing and raising his hands.

The other man smiled. "Yeah? To be honest I don't give a rats. I got orders and I'm gonna carry them out."

Andy joined them on Jed's boat. He carried a coil of thin rope and dropped it at his feet. He looked around the deck area then turned to the other man. "Where the hell are we gonna tie him up, Les?"

Les peered around for a moment, "There." He nodded at the tower of crab pots. "The cleats in the deck. That should keep him secure." Les looked at the frightened old man, pulled a pen out of his pocket and stepped over to Jed.

"First things first," he said, offering the pen and contract to Jed. "Please sign."

"Why?"

Les pushed the gun against Jed's temple. "Because I asked nicely."

Jed jumped a little and grabbed for the pen and paper. He scribbled his moniker on the page and handed it back. "Okay, I've done what you want, now you can leave me alone."

Les smiled. "Nuh. You're going down. Mr. Kirchebner doesn't want any loose ends." He turned to Andy, "Well, tie him up."

Andy went to grab Jed's hands; the old man was quick and punched Andy in the face. The younger thug fell heavily grabbing at his nose.

Les stepped in and smacked Jed in the side of the face with the gun.

The fisherman dropped to the deck with a sickening crack from his old knees. His face a mess of blood from a deep cut across his cheek. He stayed still. His consciousness fading away. Through the fog he heard the two thugs argue.

"You didn't need to do that," said Andy, "I would have had him."

"Shut up and tie him down, he'll be dead soon anyway," Les said. He turned towards Andy and chuckled, "Wait till I tell the boys at the gym you got decked by an old man."

"Shut up."

Jed felt his hands and feet pulled together before the darkness finally claimed him.

Water lapping against his face brought Jed back to awareness. He was lying on the deck, trussed up like a turkey. There was an inch of water on the deck.

Strange, pumps should have kicked in by now.

The sound of an engine nearby grabbed his attention. He looked around and set eyes on the other boat. It all came back. The larger thug, Les, looked over the railing at him, a broad grin on his face.

"You bastard," shouted Jed, "I'll get loose and I'll find you."

Les chuckled and shouted back. "No way old man. You're going down. Nobody but the crabs will know where you are."

Jed saw the reality of his situation. The water lapped over the side of the sinking boat. It was going down fast. He pulled at his bonds, but only succeeded in tightening them. Jed knew was going to die. Instead of panicking, a quiet calm resolve came over his mind. He looked back at the over-muscled thug.

"Let me tell you this, sonny," he said, "My name is Crùbag. We are named after the sea. Together we are strong and like the crab, if you cut off a claw it grows back stronger and ready for vengeance. It may not be me that finds you. It may not be tomorrow, but when it happens you will know."

As he shouted the last words, a ripple of water flooded his mouth. He coughed and spluttered the last sentence out.

On the other boat, Les was in fits of laughter. He saluted the old man. "I can't wait. Should be a fun reunion," he shouted before turning away.

Les' boat roared into life and powered away, leaving Jed to his fate.

"Good Morning Australia, I'm Donna Harbrow, and you're watching *Australia Today*. This morning we are very pleased to welcome one of Australia's most successful property developers, Mr. Douglas Kirchebner. As we have been following, Kirchebner Developments have undertaken a large program of redevelopment of the Suffolk Inlet area on the southern New South Wales coast."

Donna turned to her left, where Douglas Kirchebner sat, resplendent in an expensive blue suit. "After two long years of construction, it's not long now before opening day, is it Mr. Kirchebner?"

Douglas held up a hand. "Doug, please call me Doug, Mr. Kirchebner was my father."

They both laughed.

"Yes, Donna, we are very excited by the way things have progressed. We welcome everyone and have made sure that there are activities to suit all ages and tastes."

Donna held up a thin pamphlet and opened it to the glossy spread inside. She pointed out various photographs and read the blurb. "There's golf, tennis, snorkelling, fishing, water skiing, mountain biking. Wow. It sounds wonderful, I think I'd like to come when it opens," she said.

"And you and your audience are more than welcome. We'll be open all year round," Douglas said.

The TV screen went dark as Douglas pushed the button on the remote and dropped it onto the side table next to the couch.

The gentle lilt of a piece of soft classical music wafted through the room.

He turned towards his guest. Her blonde hair flowed down her naked back as she gyrated and danced in the cool breeze wafting in through the open doorway beyond. The sound of waves pounding the beach filtered in on the salt smell of the sea.

"Didn't you like our interview," Donna asked.

Douglas smiled, more at the sight of the moonbeams playing across her supple curves than the insipid interview. "It was fine. Everything I needed it to say," he said.

Donna stopped dancing and stared towards him. "I could have been harder on you," she said. "Made it into a hard-hitting investigative piece."

"What would you investigate?" he asked.

"The rumours."

"Rumours?"

"About the previous owner of this land."

Douglas chuckled. "Rumours. Lies put about by my enemies. Jed Crùbag accepted a small fortune for this place. He went off somewhere new and is probably living the high life on some island in the pacific."

"That's what I tell them," Donna said. "But some just won't believe."

"It's good to see we still have an *understanding* between us. You keep reporting the facts I tell you, and if anyone gets pushy, then tell them they should come and talk to me. I'll put them straight."

"Or you'll get that meathead Les to put them straight?"

Douglas smiled. "Well there's more than one way to skin a cat."

Donna sashayed across the polished wooden floor and straddled him. "There are more important things to worry about tonight," she said, kissing him full on the lips.

Neither noticed the light from the moon cut out as something large skittered away across the beautifully manicured lawn beyond.

Andy watched the waves roll gently onto the small sandy beach. The developers had cut into the rocky cliff and levelled it out to create a safe and suitable area for families to bring their children for a swim.

The bright full moon glinted off the water, its reflection breaking up as the ripples built into waves and broke onto the white sands.

Despite the warm night, a chill ran up Andy's back as the idyllic setting brought back a flood of memories of the previous owner. He pictured the poor man shackled to the deck of his boat as it sank beneath the waves.

Andy never signed up for murder. Working for Mr. Kirchebner was better that the crappy jobs he'd taken in the past, and some of the things he'd been asked to do at times were on the wrong side of the moral compass, but he considered murder one step too far. He had threatened to leave but soon realised that was a one-way trip with no happy ending. Mr. Kirchebner covered Andy's palm with more money that he could hope to earn in a year, and when Les whispered in his ear his desire for escape turned into a life dedicated to his boss. The alternative being a short life devoted to hiding.

As he slipped off his t-shirt, he thought of the cross he had to bear. It was his and his alone. There was consolation in the fact everything had been Les' idea. Not much, but it helped him sleep at night.

Standing up, he dropped his t-shirt on the sand, kicked off his thongs and stepped towards the shoreline. The resort was almost finished. Within a week the place would be teeming with tourists and visitors. This was one of the last occasions he was ever going to have the beach to himself.

The sand squeaked under his feet as he walked towards the water. Clean sand. Carted in from one of the nearby beaches, known throughout the land as the whitest sand in the country. It wouldn't last long. Kids and parents would dump their crap and leave it for the help to clean up.

Andy wanted to remember the place the way it felt at this moment in time. He didn't expect to return for a while, Mr. Kirchebner had other plans and new resorts to build. Andy just hoped the owners would be more compliant than Mr. Crùbag.

The water ran its icy fingers through him as he stepped into the waves, dived in and swam out for a good fifty metres. The cold, brought an alertness to his mind with its chilly touch, cooling his overworked muscles and mind. Powering on for another couple of hundred metres, Andy swore he could feel a sweat breaking out that was immediately sucked off his body by the cold water.

With his attention focused on his swimming, Andy failed to notice the two grey triangles emerge slowly from the depths behind him. They kept pace while he swam and sunk quickly out of sight when he stopped to catch his breath. Andy glanced back at the distant beach, then to the far horizon. He decided to head out for another hundred metres or so.

Then he saw it.

The grey fin scythed out of the water in front of him and dived out of sight soon after. Andy almost screamed in terror. Turning for safety, his heart stopped when another fin appeared between him and the beach.

The grey points rose out of the water and dipped back below in a synchronised pattern, blocking off any escape.

When Andy moved in one direction; a fin closed in forcing him backwards. He stayed, treading water, trying not to splash too hard in case it caused the sharks to attack.

The two fins circled, orbiting him in opposite directions.

Andy hoped they would get bored or realise he wasn't anything they really wanted to eat and swim away. His wish was answered when both fins disappeared below the surface. He took his chance and powered on towards the shore.

Too late.

Something snagged his leg. He thought it was a piece of driftwood, but it left a strange lingering pain. He stopped. The cold water numbed the pain, but it was still there. Thinking he might be bleeding from a small cut, Andy reached down towards his knee and felt for his leg. He was rewarded with only the jagged ends of splintered bone and jellied muscle.

Another tug.

He brought his arm up out of the water. Blood sprayed from the stump of his wrist. Where his hand should be, only bone and meat remained.

He screamed out across the quiet sea.

Another tug.

Andy shrieked. He thrashed around with his one remaining hand in a desperate attempt to escape. His mind clouded, threatening to cast him into the blackness. Only his terror kept him conscious.

Pain ignited across his body again. His other leg was gone and with it his ability to stay afloat. He sunk beneath the waves. His eyes peering through the murky gloom and spying the cause of his demise. Speeding through the dark was a grey and white shape, with two baleful circles of black staring directly into his own eyes.

His last sight was a mouth full of razor-sharp triangles of death.

The infinity pool looked out over the resort complex and the expanse of ocean beyond. Ripples extended across the salt water, sending reflected moonlight in all directions and lapping over the edge to fall away from sight. Ripples that originated from the gyrating couple on the other side of the pool. Moon beams glinted off the sweaty muscular back and buttocks of the man and the pair of long slender legs jutted out of the water and wrapped around him.

As Les grunted in time with his thrusting, the woman let out small groans of delight. Both were ignorant of the beautiful scene spread out before them. As his movements became more frantic, his grunts increased in volume to match his speed. The woman's groans matched Les', both increasing in volume until she screamed, and he let out a satisfied sigh of relief.

Their movements slowed and they parted. A wide grin on his satisfied face, Les leaned against the side of the pool, stretched his arms wide and bent his head back to look at the ceiling. The light reflecting off the water cast small patches of white above him.

"That was wonderful Les," the woman said as she leaned over and kissed him on the chest.

"Yeah, wasn't it," Les said, obviously pleased with himself. He wrapped one arm around her shoulder and closed his eyes. "If you hang on for another few minutes Sharon, we can have a second round."

Sharon grimaced to herself, then pulled away. "I have to pee."

"Not in here you don't. Only gets cleaned once a week."

As Sharon stepped out of the pool, water cascaded off her slender frame and ran down the nearby drain. She grabbed one of the white, fluffy towels from the towel rail and threw it around herself. As she started to move away, Les' voice piped up. "Get me a beer while you're at it, hey?"

She stopped walking, his request hitting her like a barb, then Sharon remembered why she was there and concentrated on that as she disappeared into the bowels of the penthouse. Les had ordered the *Girlfriend Experience*, and Sharon didn't want word getting back that she hadn't delivered to the maximum expected. The money from this job would be good, but reputation guaranteed more jobs.

Les laid back, his thoughts fading away to sleep, the water gently lapping against his chest, sloughing the sweat away. A light breeze blew up from the beach, the hairs on his arms and chest rose in response.

Below, in the main garden area of the resort, a large shadowy figure moved amongst the foliage, its feet scraping across the narrow concrete paths that criss-crossed the grassed zones.

The water lapped over the edge of the pool in a continuous cascading fall. The collector at the base sent the water into the tiny pump which brought it back to the main pool. For a moment the pump whirred with effort as something joined the water within the pipes.

The outlet stopped discharging water as two long grey objects wriggled their way through the pipe and slithered silently into the pool. They took a moment to regain their bearings and swam towards the man reposing at the far end of the pool.

Les' eyes shot open as a bolt of pain ran up his leg. He looked around thinking the girl had returned and tried to arouse him again. She was nowhere to be seen. He looked down into the pool. A dark cloud encased his leg below the water's surface.

What the fuck?

He saw a dark shadow dart towards him. His stomach roared with fire as something bit deep into the muscles. Blood seeped from the wound enshrouding his midriff in a mist of dark water.

The fuck? Someone's stabbed me.

Les stood and peered into the water. "Who the fuck's there?" He stepped away from the wall towards the middle of the pool. The water reached up to his chest, but he could plainly see the torn skin on his stomach and the blood that leaked out of him. His hands closed into fists and he splayed his legs in a fighting stance, ready to attack the interloper. "I'm gonna fix you up good."

The lights shining upwards gave the entire area a strange ghostly white glow, making it difficult for Les to make out any details in the water. Then he saw them. Two long grey shadows zoomed through the water. One turned towards him. "Shit." He turned and waded as fast as he could for the edge, but it was on him before he took two steps.

Below the water, the eel sized up Les and darted forward. Its target, the floppy, soft meat floating limply in the water below the harder flesh above.

Les screamed as his manhood was ripped asunder. A dark fog of blood poured from the wound. His hands went to his wound, trying in vain to staunch the flow of blood.

Beneath the surface, the other eel darted forward. This one was different. As soon as it latched onto Les' thick buttock muscle it let a full electrical discharge course into its prey.

Les' arms shot out as the shock hit him. His heart stopped for a moment, seizing his body in the grip of a death. He dropped to his knees and fell forward into the water. The first eel seized its opportunity and drove forward, ripping a chunk of flesh from Les' face.

Les peered up through the cloud of blood. The eel floated before him. In his mind he saw the grizzled face of the old man and heard his words of revenge.

We are of the sea. We are stronger together.

Les felt the second eel latch on once more. A shocking bolt of pain arced through his chest, seizing his heart in its grip and squeezing until it stilled forever.

The eels pulled back and attacked the prone body, gorging on the henchman's flesh and turning the pool into a thin soup of blood and bits of Les.

Sharon walked back from the kitchen holding a beer in one hand and a bottle of champagne in the other. She saw Les' body floating amidst a miasma of gore and shrieked in horror. The beer dropped from her grasp and bounced once on the tiles before exploding on the second bounce.

All the girls had heard the rumours about Les' employer, it didn't put any of them off, but they were wary just in case things turned sour. Sharon looked at Les' body and realised things had definitely gone sour.

I ain't sticking around for this shit.

She looked around for any obvious attackers, holding the champagne bottle like a club for protection. When the area seemed quiet, she quickly found the money Les had promised, snatched it up and stowed it away in her purse before grabbing her clothes and racing for the exit.

She took one look back towards the pool.

Should I at least call the cops?

She thought for a second and shook her head.

Too many questions.

Self-preservation kicked in and Sharon was gone before the door clicked shut.

The dark shadow outside watched with satisfaction before moving on.

Terrence Kirchebner walked around his domain. He was elated. His father had financed the entire construction phase, but this was to be his to control and manage. It would be a gold mine and set him up for life.

The four-storey edifice ringed the area in a semi-circle of glass and concrete, consisting of two hundred apartments. Only the stairway lights blazed, giving it a strange ethereal glow in the darkness of the night. Terrence stared at it with excitement. Each apartment would be filled with families for several months over summer. The thought of all the money pouring in sent his mind reeling.

In front of the building sat several close-cropped grassed areas, ready for young feet to run over, separated by narrow, stone paved concrete paths. A thick canopy of tropical bamboos, yucca and cordyline hid the apartment block from view at ground level, giving the tourists a sense of isolation and, in turn, privacy to the ground floor units. The paths led off down to the tiny man-made beach and the shiny sea beyond.

Several penthouses stood alone and far away, ringing the inlet itself. These had the best position and the best views and were reserved for very *special* guests or those that could afford the best. Looking up the hill, Terrence saw dull lights shining in two of the apartments, the rest, including his own were dark.

A large pool sat off in the distance, looking barren with all the pool chairs and tables all packed away until the opening. For now, the entire resort was here just for himself, his father, and the two thugs that never left his father's side.

Terrence walked along a path to the pool. He felt like a quick swim, but that meant returning to his penthouse to change, and he wasn't the kind to go skinny dipping. Especially if that big lug was watching. He unconsciously stared up at the penthouses again. Les' pool shone with a dull glow. He snapped his attention away. Terrence had seen the girl arrive and didn't need Les catching him looking. There'd be jeering accusations of his perving thrown at him behind his father's back.

As Terrence stepped through a small gap in the line of palms, the sight shocked him to the core.

The small building that housed the towels and pool chairs was a shattered ruin. Chairs, towels, shards of wood and brick littered the area. It looked as if it had been swept aside by a cyclone.

Terrence ran to the side of the building and saw a path of destruction, with shattered trees and shrubs lying askew all the way down to the little dock that was the last reminder of the previous owner.

This was where the old man's house had stood. They had even used some of the footings and bricks. His father was always one to avoid extra expense where he could.

He pulled out his phone and dialled Les' number. Within a few seconds he was answered by a recorded voice asking him to leave a message. He dialled Andy's number, the same result. His eyes were drawn back to Les' penthouse.

The idiot is in.

Terrence checked his watch and thought for a moment.

Andy usually swims at the beach this time of night. Les it is then. I don't care if he's bonking his brains out, we've got a problem.

Terrence thumped on the penthouse door then put an ear to the wood and listened. Nothing. No movement. No voices. No music.

He banged harder, wary not to get carried away and damage the wood.

Again nothing.

He pulled out his wallet and extracted his passkey.

Les might kill me for this, but I'm still the boss, gotta remember that.

Terrence pushed the door open and hurried into the main area. The crunch of glass under foot pulled him up short. He peered around the darkened room and saw the light from the pool just outside. Then the shape floating face down in a cloud of darkness in the middle of the pool.

He took two steps forward, glass splintering beneath his shoes, and stared closer at the figure. The distinctive shape of a well-muscled back told him it was his father's bodyguard. The dark pool of water around Les suggested his position wasn't natural.

"Fuck. What have you done now Les?"

Peering around the room, Terrence tried to glean details from the clues spread about. The glass bottle. Brown. Probably a beer stubby. On the counter sat a bottle of champagne. A white towel lay discarded nearby. Another sat folded over by the pool.

The girl? Terrence shook his head. *No. It'd take a lot more than her to take down Les.*

He pulled out his phone and dialled "000", before the operator could answer he blurted out, "This is Terrence Kirchebner at the Crùbag Resort in Suffolk Inlet. We've got a murder. I need the police and an ambulance."

As the operator asked for details he snapped, "Just do what I said," and hung up.

Do I tell Dad? No. I'm the boss. Find Andy. We'll get these fucks. Then I'll tell Dad.

Terrence jogged down to the beach, peering round every few seconds just in case the killers were hiding nearby. He was confident he was safe, the heavy weight of Les' pistol in his hand gave him that feeling. Still, he was wary of an ambush. The path lighting only provided a meagre glow, partly for ambiance but mostly to keep the costs down.

He reached the sand and stepped out into the open. Small waves washed up onto the shore with the lulling sound that normally sent him to sleep.

The design team had worked magic. The little beach was cut out of the jagged cliffs and formed a small semi-circular area lined with bamboo and palms that provided both a beautiful panorama and a bit of shade from the bright afternoon sun.

Nestled beneath a tall palm tree, Terrence found Andy's towel and phone. He saw a thin line of footsteps leading down to the water's edge and peered out into the gloom trying to catch sight of the bodyguard.

Damn. Nothing. He could be anywhere.

He stepped towards the shore and stared out towards the horizon, hoping to catch a glimpse of light against the dark sea. There was nothing.

A deep voice boomed from out of the darkness. It seemed to surround Terrence making him unsure if it was just inside his head. "He is gone," it said.

"Who's there?" he said, bringing the gun up in one trembling hand and turning around to search for the voice's origin.

The voice thundered again. "The one you seek is gone. Lost to the sea forever."

Terrence stepped towards the gloom at the edge of the beach. He was sure he could see something dark against the shadows. "Where are you?"

"I am where I need to be."

"What?"

Then Terrence saw it. Movement in the undergrowth. A glint of moon flared off something shiny. He stepped forward, aiming the pistol at the shadow. "Why did you kill Les?"

"The law of the sea. He killed for no reason. He must die."

"What? Who did he kill?"

"He that lived in this place. He that was one with us."

Terrence shook his head, fear and confusion growing in his mind. "What are you talking about?"

"The last of his line. The last of those that were of the sea."

Terrence finally realised who the voice was talking about. The old man. Jed Crùbag. The man his father had bought the inlet and its surrounds off. "You mean old Jed? We paid him a lot of money. My father said he moved away, retired."

The voice grew in volume, the words ejected with a tinge of threat. "Your father lies. The old man was one with us. Now he lives with us forever at the bottom of the sea. You killed him."

Terrence stepped back in fear, "I didn't kill him. I didn't know anything about it. It was my father, not me."

"Then your father will know loss. Just like the old man. Then he will join the old man in death."

"No," shouted Terrence. He raised the gun and aimed at the shadow. It moved forward and the moonlight flashed across its features. Baleful black eyes peered out at Terrence.

"Oh, my God!" Terrence shrieked in horror at the sight.

The dark figure struck out. Terrence was lifted off his feet, his finger squeezing the trigger. The gun fired, the report deafening in the still night. The bullet went wide. The young Kirchebner was thrown across the beach. The gun flew from his grasp, as he bounced once on the hard-packed sand and finished face-down in the gently lapping water. The gun splashed down metres away and sank to the bottom.

Bubbles burst around his head and he reared up out of the water dragging air into his lungs, only to scream them raw.

His head was covered with small octopi, each with bright blue rings decorating their legs and body. A single bite from this species could render a man unconscious, several bites were fatal. A dozen creatures, all biting at once, sent Terrence to his death within moments.

He fell back into the sea and lay still.

Douglas Kirchebner sat back on the leather couch. He looked out across the resort and smiled at the peaceful scene of moonlight and a calm sea.

This was as close as he ever wanted to get to the water. He was happy to create a place of pleasure for others, but the thought of entering that vast ocean filled him with terror. Always had.

His brother had died when they were kids. Drowned on a simple holiday at the beach. Playing together, they had waded out too deep, beyond their depth. A sudden wave and he was alone. They found his brother's body the next day. The loss had stayed with him ever since.

A cool breeze wafted in from the open patio doors and drifted across his naked body, awash with sweat from his recent dalliance with TV's golden girl.

He shivered slightly, partly from the cold, partly from remembrance of his brother, then stretched out his arms, and slid a little down the coach, letting his head lay back on the top. The dank smell of rotting seaweed drifted into the suite. Douglas' nose twitched in revulsion.

It's the sea. It always stinks. Another reason I hate it so much.

His eyes snapped open as a wet thumping noise pierced the silence. Confused, he looked around for the source.

At his feet was the decapitated head of his son. It was covered in a mess of welts and lumps, and lay staring up at him with a look of absolute horror forever fixed on its face.

48

Douglas cried out. "Terrence. What have they done?"

Donna, naked and glistening, raced into the room. "What's wrong Dougy?" she said before shrieking out in pain.

When Douglas saw what had hold of her, he screamed in terror.

Donna was suspended in mid-air, held between the massive pincers of a gigantic crab. Its black eyes poked forward on their stalks and stared at Douglas. Its mandibles flickered in anticipation.

Douglas frantically searched for an escape. The room only had two exits, out across the patio and the corridor from the bedroom that Donna had used. From where it stood, the giant crustacean controlled both.

Donna screamed out to him in a plaintive cry. "Dougy! help me, *please*!"

The crab squeezed tighter, the claw cutting deep into her, Donna screamed as blood poured down her midriff. She coughed once, a red froth spewed forth and ran down her chest.

Doug took one furtive step towards her. A deep voice boomed across the room. He stopped, grabbing at his ears with both hands to try to silence it.

"You killed he who was of the sea. You must join him."

Douglas looked at the crab. The voice was coming from the creature. "This is impossible," he gasped.

"We live. We see all. We will have our revenge."

Douglas peered around himself again. He moved towards the bedroom doorway, the crab spread its claws wide, blocking it. It was hopeless, he was trapped. Douglas dropped to his knees. "I'll give you anything you want."

"You have nothing we desire. There is only justice."

"Let the girl go and we can work this out."

"She is nothing." The claw thrust forward and squeezed shut.

Donna gave one last scream before her torso parted in a spray of blood and organs. The two halves flopped to the shiny, wooden floor.

"Christ!" shouted Douglas, his eyes widened in horror and his thoughts turned to escape again. Grabbing a nearby chair, he threw it at the window. It bounced off, the glass fracturing but remaining intact.

Fucking double glazing.

His moment's hesitation was a moment too much. The crab's claw exploded through the glass, sending the sound of splintering glass through the room.

"There is no escape."

Douglas turned to see the crab right standing next to him, its pincer ready to clamp around him. He dodged backwards, but the crab was too quick. The pain was excruciating as the pincer closed around his midriff and compressed until he could hardly wriggle.

The crab lifted him to eye height. "This land was tended by those of the sea. We of the sea are stronger together. Your greed took the last, now there are none. You will not replace them, but you will join them." The crab backed out of the room, glass, steel and brickwork slid off its carapace and crashed to the floor.

Douglas cried out as glass splinters nicked his face, leaving wet trails of fresh blood.

Turning sideways, the crab set off across the grassed area, its weight digging grooves into the fresh turf.

"What are you doing? Where are you taking me?"

"You will serve a greater purpose." It was heading for the beach, to the sea, to the water.

Douglas began to yell and thump his fists on the thick shell of the creature's claws. The crab ignored him and carried on, reaching the beach swiftly and scuttling across the sand.

When the water touched Douglas' naked feet, he cried out "No, not that, anything but that."

The great crustacean plunged into the rippling waves. As the water rose up his body, Douglas let out one final scream that cut off as the crab disappeared below the surface.

About the Author:

Stephen is an IT Geek, writer, actor, film maker and Taekwondo Black Belt based in Canberra Australia. He has been writing for over twenty years and has completed a couple of dodgy novels, sixteen feature length screenplays and dozens of short stories and scripts.

Stephen's scripts TITAN, Dark are the Woods, Control *and* Death Spores *have found success in international screenwriting competitions with a win, two runner-up and two top ten finishes.*
His horror stories have featured in various anthologies including: Sproutlings; Hells Bells; Trickster's Treats #1, #2 and #3; Shades of Santa; Below the Stairs; Behind the Mask; Beyond the Infinite; Beside the Seaside; The Body Horror Book; Anemone Enemy; Petrified Punks; Beginnings; Sea of Secrets, Demonic Carnival; Deep Space; A Tribute to H.G. Wells; What If?; Through Death's Door *and* Coffins and Dragons.

Over forty of his drabbles have been accepted by Blood Song Books; Black Hare Press; Fantasia Divinity and ThingsInTheWell.

Several of his Sherlock Holmes pastiches have been accepted for inclusion in anthologies published by Belanger Books and MX Publishing.

You can catch Stephen at his Facebook page:
https://www.facebook.com/stephenherczegauthor

THE RIVER S CHILD

Kel E. Fox

Whispers of the wind in twisted branches tell of autumn.
Raindrops meld with my rushing body. Winter turns them into
soft beautiful snowflakes that pile up on my banks, or around a
sleeping animal, seeping the life out of it.

People think I am indiscriminate with the lives I take, that
anyone who dares get too close will be swept off and drowned, but
that is not true. I do not take children.

George Swinston is not a child, and he plans to dam me.

I froth and roil, rapid with rain and snow, but not where I pass
Riverdale Manor. There I widen and wallow with the flattened
valley, a sunlit reprieve from the dense forests to the north or
deep southern ravines. George grew up in the city; he has never
splashed in my shallow waters, listened to the wind sigh on a good
day or felt the rush of running wildly down the hillside and

skidding to a muddy stop on my sun-warmed shore, arms a-flailing. Although George owns the land, his mother-in-law still lives here, harbouring a bitter frigidity far chillier than the winter wind could manage, and not even I am immune to her nature. Already gentled by the valley, I slow to a crawl, so still and quiet that the season takes me too and I freeze. I am trapped here, in this cold, hushed place. I hear everything.

A rabbit approaches upstream, where I am just barely frozen over. It tests the ice with a tentative paw.

Hooves clatter up the cobblestone driveway towards the manor and I long to know who is visiting, but the wind is not speaking to me. It is not speaking to anyone today—it has days like that.

I wait.

The parlour overlooks my banks, close enough for me to listen. George sloshes brandy into glasses. I recognise the voice of the local mayor. "The council will not approve it, George."

"They will. See here." There is rustling of papers, sounds of fingers tapping on the table and men making ponderous grunts.

Finally, the mayor sets down his glass with his heavy hands. "You have two days."

Upstream, the rabbit takes one step too far. It slips, sliding onto the ice, and frantically scrabbles back towards the soil, but the ice here is thin.

CRACK.

I take the rabbit. The wind will moan tomorrow.

George's children arrive the next afternoon. I cannot hear them coming along the drive, but the wind is up today, and it tells me everything. It buffets the carriage, moaning, and the youngest child cries while his sister, Juliet, fusses over him.

"Don't fret, Henry." She pulls out her handkerchief and dries her brother's cheeks. "It's only for a week, while Father finishes his business."

Henry's seven. He knows how long a week at Grandmother's is.

George is out, pacing my shores, testing the ice. I could crack it. I press up against the weakest part. The ice strains. George stops. He stamps his foot. I push. Before I can get the ice to split, he turns and walks back to the edge.

Grandmother makes tea in the parlour. The old house is quiet, except for the wind whining around its eaves.

"Father says the river is frozen," says Henry, the trauma of a week away from home forgotten in the face of a new adventure. "Can we go skating?"

"Tomorrow." Grandmother gazes into her tea leaves.

Snow falls outside, silencing the creaking wind.

Shortly after sunrise, Henry pads across the dusty bedroom floor and pulls aside a velveteen curtain. Snow glistens under the cold winter sun as far as he can see, but I steal his gaze: I sparkle, crystalline and vast, right below his window. He digs his skates out of his suitcase and races to the dining hall. Juliet has already eaten.

Grandmother watches from the steps as the children skate upstream, in and out of sight. George is on the opposite bank with string and thin wooden stakes and he waves at them to go back, where the ice is strong, but Grandmother's cold proximity keeps them safe. They circle around, carving ellipses and figure-eights. I swirl, dancing beneath them, eddying pools with tiny bubbles trailing like effervescent joy.

That evening, Grandmother reads her tea leaves. She is not gifted, not at this, but Juliet pays attention and it warms the old woman's voice. Henry falls asleep in his chair. Horseshoes ring in the courtyard and George excuses himself into the night. Grandmother goes to bed with an extra quilt, the one crocheted by her daughter: the one she hasn't used since the funeral.

Two men, heavy bags slung over their shoulders, follow George down to my edge. George carries a long coil of fuse wire.

I beat against the ice as they walk onto it. I will drown them before they can set fire to my banks. But they cross and climb the opposite side, stumbling up the gentle hill. The two men lay charges at the stakes while George runs the wires. It will be a landslide, a natural disaster. The council will have no choice but to approve George's proposal. He'll be doing them a favour.

Henry wakes in his bed, itching under the old woollen blanket. He gets up and peers out the window. Moonlight glints on the patterns he and Juliet carved in the ice. Struck by its beauty, Henry realises that this is the first time he has been truly aware, the beginning of a person, no longer an infant driven only by the animal instinct to thrive. Heart quickening with anticipation, he stuffs his bed with pillows and steals out, skates in hand.

The explosives are laid. George makes his way back across the ice towards the house with his wire, skidding and slipping in his snow-packed boots.

Henry sits in a shadow on the cold stone steps to tie his laces. He pauses; he will be in terrible trouble with Grandmother, but I shine alluringly, despite myself. I don't want to make trouble either, yet the desire to dance again is too much to bear, and I feel his longing. His gift is dancing too.

Juliet cannot sleep. She pauses at Henry's door; he appears huddled under the blankets. She goes downstairs to make herself tea.

George is almost at the bank when he hears the unmistakable sound of ice splintering, spiderweb fractures forming an inescapable net. He knows the ice is thick here, but not that I am pounding it. Breath fogging the frigid air, George makes it across and runs the wire along the riverbank, past the house. He doesn't look up from his treacherous footing. He doesn't see Henry.

Henry's skate snags as he shuffles down the bank, too absorbed in his own excitement to notice the dark shape of his father upstream, or the men across the river.

I feel a thrum in the wire as the skate tugs it across the ice.

Juliet turns her cup three times, upside-down on its saucer.

Henry shakes his foot to release it. Perhaps he thinks it a twig, or a root. On the other side, tugged by Henry's skate, one of the incendiaries tumbles onto my frozen surface.

The men stand back while George lights the fuse.

Juliet's brow furrows. She tilts the cup towards the lamplight, understanding what her Grandmother cannot.

George sees the misplaced explosive. His breath catches— blowing up the ice here might raise questions. The landslide must bury the evidence.

Henry steps out onto the ice. He glides like a swan, the breeze tickling his face, every sense alive and aware as he makes art. Still as a pond, I dare not dance with him. If I can hold up the ice, I will.

Juliet drops the teacup. The heirloom shatters on the parlour floor.

George races to cut the wire. He sees his son.

Henry skates over the fragmenting ice. I hold still and plead with the moonlight to glimmer downriver, to lead Henry away.

George doesn't reach the wire. He slips in the snow and slithers onto the ice, into the fractured net. I could break it now and swallow him. Him and Henry both.

"Henry!" Juliet's anguish splits the bitter air. George's cry is wordless.

I don't take children. But a cloud drifts over the moon and with the pop-pop-pop of a fireworks finale, the explosives ignite.

CRACK.

Grandmother turns in her too-warm bed and the wind begins to howl.

About the Author:

Kel E Fox ran an apothecary in a past life, was a stage technician before she finally embraced writing in this life and hopes to be a wizard in the next. She writes an eclectic mix of speculative fiction and is working on her debut release 'Darkhaven', *the first of a YA fantasy saga about a girl who gets struck by lightning, develops superpowers, stumbles into a global conspiracy and meets an alien god all in the same day.*

Kel lives in Perth, Australia with her life (and ballroom dancing) partner, two lazy cats and a wilful young Alaskan Malamute named after Nighteyes.

See more at <u>kelefox.com</u> *or find her on socials @kelelizabethfox*

Exacting Revenge

Barbara Smith

Flickering light dances across the flat surface of water before me

The new moon hovering above the distant eastern horizon shares a pale light

Transcending expectations

My focus is drawn toward crystal shaped shades.

A low, white, wash rolls closer to the shoreline.

You appear with a wide gait

Photographically detailed

With recognisable superiority and the colour of the sun.

I watch as the sand near my feet draws the wash downward

Downward into the unknown

Disappearing to the inner world of your transparent life.

Your superiority envelops my soul.

The time has come to let go

Of long processed attitudes

And the predilection to self-harm the mental state

Feigning strength to overcome internal weakness

Hiding the truth from those close at hand.

My savoir-faire has been directed by your morbid words

My adaptability in crisis situations

My strength is in the mask I wear

A mask I now remove, revealing the inner mechanisms.

Here I am exposed, apprehensive, following you into the depths

I am wary of falling within reach

if clawed feet should stumble along the crystal pathway.

My journey stops here

No longer giving all

The finale is close

Desire to destroy is rapturous

The return of a Cimmerian existence begins

With your farewell performance disappearing to the distance

I will try words of wisdom at the end

Before your world goes blind.

About the Author:

Barbara has worked in teaching at Universities for many years and published her debut picture book, 'Otis Paul & Harry the Hairy Echidna' *in 2019. Having tried her hand at many things, from spinning wool to building an earth house, she now illustrates children's stories, writes in varied genres, and spends time with her beautiful family. You can read her collective poetry on her blog Lifeandbeyondblog@wordpress.com, where she adds some skills as a photographer. You can follow her on twitter @BarbAnn.*

THE ANTHROPOLOGY OF DIVING

Brianna Bullen

Diving used to be peaceful.

When Jenni was a child, she would spend all day in and with the waves, gently being buoyed by its tides before going under. Beneath the surface, its pull visible, she would spend whole afternoons suspended in the ocean, going up only for air. She'd learned to swim as soon as her muscles allowed for it. Her mother would take her into the ocean to learn its tides and feelings.

Her earliest memories were of gentle blue, folding over green and white light. She was safe in her mother's arms, held close and yet able to explore the water with her own hands and feet. Her mother used to say her giggle matched the gurgle of the sea. She'd been criticized for the casualness (some would say recklessness) with which she'd introduced her child to the sea, but she barely cared. As DolTHINK Corps' best diver, these grumblings never made it beyond pithy comment. Baptized in salt-spray, the smell that came with storms and sand was encoded into Jenni's nostrils.

It had been a gentle childhood, the only damage the frizz the saltwater gave her hair and the occasional shock at being dunked underwater. Beneath the waves, she could see life. In utero, amniotic fluid distorted blue, she watched her brothers and sisters in the fish swimming by, the seaweed that spread out in Rorschach approximations, and the occasional seal gliding by with the virtuosity and improvisations of a jazz dancer. In these moments, she embodied stillness, limbs moving in response to the ocean's tugs. Her legs would kick, uncanny extensions made slow as if watching a film in fractions.

Crab hunting used to be a lucrative profession, but these days— due to high extinction rates—it was frowned upon, viewed as morally wrong, and illegal everywhere but around the island. Yet the demand was still high. Not high enough to transfer across into respect and money, but enough to keep them employed. The sheer amount of money required for a crab license, and the quota entitlement under that license, meant extra work to move beyond losing money.

Yet, her mother thought it was worth the risk, time, and expense. It was the only job she could get that could support her entire family. They were poorer than most. so her mother had to work harder and take even higher risks than most to 'stay afloat'—a turn of phrase of great irony to a diver.

While her school friends were saving up their income for the latest technological marvels and branded styles, Jenni was busy studying and learning to mend broken things. Her father was the hardest to mend, but could be helped with attention, conversation, and pills given to them by her mother's supervisor. From where she sat, Jenni misheard their name as 'Andy D presents,' so for many years she had thought her mother's supervisor was called 'Andy D'. Broken buttons and burnt cooking were a lot easier to salvage than her father, but they were happy and the ocean was free.

She was too young to realise everything came with a cost.

That all changed when her mother died.

It was a simple death, really. Quite inane and quite pointless. Divers died all the time; caught in currents, out of oxygen, equipment malfunction, attacked by sea creatures, smashing into rocks, unable to find their way back up in the depths, decompression sickness, strokes. The bends had bent the innards of more than enough divers to take caution. Her mother proved death could happen to anyone: she was a complete expert, practical and intelligent in her dives, bringing up what seafood she could every time. She'd load up her oxygen, enough with her own breathing techniques and practices to last her six hours at a time, harvesting kilogram upon kilogram of crab-life each day, six days a week. Using the tricks she's learned through a lifetime underwater to trap the giant beasts, she would use the ocean terrain to her advantage against the crabs' bulky bodies.

On average, she would take back seventy kilograms of smaller seafood each day, plucked from the ocean as if there were an unlimited supply, alongside three of the giant beasts. Her wetsuit was technologically high-end, capable of warming itself underwater to maintain a steady mellow temperature (her skills rewarded by the company), she dived deeper and lasted longer than most others. But they were a family. She had been with them since she was eleven, diving every day of her life, not just for practical but personal purpose.

The official story had been one of tragedy, tinged with the presumed greed of those who had nothing: money overriding self-preservation and professionalism. Her mother liked to go swimming at night, usually without gear. This painted her as a deviant. She liked the danger, being surrounded by blank black nothingness. Infinity and the cold. No way up or down, letting her body and oxygen needs keep her afloat and steady, fully primal and embodied on the surface of the water. Breathing in, going under, releasing and letting herself float back up to the surface.

On the night she died, she was reported to have been doing just that when she was approached by a man who yelled across the ocean to her, wanting her help. A simple task: some fresh crab straight from the sea in exchange for enough cash to keep her family housed and fed for the week. All he'd wanted—he later claimed—was to watch the famous diver in her element, while

nobody else was around. No one who knew her bought the story—
she was too smart, not that greedy, she knew better than to dive
alone, let alone at night. But the authorities believed it. She was
found the next day, washed up like litter against the rocks. Jenni
remembered seeing her, the lifeless body alien, more wetsuit than
person, folded at odd angles around the rock. She had been
twelve at the time. Old enough, they'd said, to begin diving for
'real rewards'. Jenni had taken this to mean money and self-
respect, although they'd kept her off the official payment sheets
until she was eighteen. She felt she was an echo of her mum,
diving young to support a wounded family.

The bank had been insistent though: pay up, or you're on the
street. Her father received income that she did not, but he spent it
all on his demons. Jobs existed for those who wanted them and
those who needed them; the dangerous positions filled the latter,
those desperate enough to take them. There were those in cults
who wanted 'organic, traditional methods,' the thought of
mechanical harvesting and genetically modified (or artificially
printed) food put them on edge, even though technology had
always been used in food production. For the needs of a wealthy,
stupid few, the workers were still exploited.

Jenni knew more than the others about her mother's death:
her mother had been on edge in the weeks prior to the lethal
incident. When she'd said this to the officers, they'd assumed that
maybe there was a suicidal aspect to the story, and were even
more sure it was a closed case. But Jenni had heard her mother

raise her voice to her father, who was too stuck in his own past to hear. She's spoken about the degradation she had seen beneath the waves, the ocean's slow death. The need for the divers to stop. Not just to implement safer procedures and regulations, but to stop completely. She 'felt a monster' for continuing to hunt down a species that was on the brink. She wasn't going to do it anymore. Over a period of weeks the conversation shifted from 'they have to know' to 'they've always known.' Jenni, listening in with a cup from within their thin toilet wall, thought maybe her mother had always known about the destruction. But she had *hoped.* Jenni's mother thought the company wasn't complicit, just ignorant. That they would change if presented with statistics gathered of the creatures' precarious existence, of the damage they had done. Had spent many months of her life documenting the impacts of their practices. But of course, they had known all along. The company had not accepted her resignation, so much so that no one had written the paperwork for it. No records. No evidence. Her mum was going to go public.

And then she'd discovered more: toxicity levels within the crabs. The alien inhabitants of the sea were radiating killer-particles. The crabs had come on a comet—not so much crabs, but it was simpler for the public to accept them as 'space crabs' than to conceptualize them as alien organisms with their own systems and intelligence. Simpler for the company to sell them based on the idea they were no different to earth crabs. The slow death of the ocean would convert to a slow death of the customer. She was not going to let it be a quiet death.

Hers had been subdued, where it should have been loud.

Her mother had needed to talk to others about the destruction, but there was no one to trust. It wasn't fair to unload it on her child. Jenni couldn't do anything. Just feel afraid. Although maybe her mother had spoken to someone about it, and that had led to her demise.

Jenni was not going to make the same mistake. She only wanted to dive. She loved the ocean, she would die for it, but she wasn't going to stick her neck out for it. She was stuck caring for her dad and herself; she didn't have the luxury of caring for an ecosystem, as much as she revered it. No other diver seemed to.

One of the women, had dived for over sixty years, her skin age-worn and water-marked, bloated as wet paper. Martina was simultaneously the coolest and most terrifying woman Jenni had ever met, as coarse as the waves and as able to roll with whatever crap was placed on it. She refused to drink, but was the hardest partying octogenarian in the island area, capable of dancing into the morning and then diving two hours later. This lifestyle eased up after a fractured hip, and yet she continued to dive. Jenni couldn't speak for everyone—who could tell the needs or motivations of a stranger, when her own were still so opaque to herself?—but she suspected Martina was as tied to the ocean as her mother had been. Although poorly-paying, risky and technically illegal, their jobs were an open secret, and nobody dared cross

71

them with disrespect. Jenni was afraid that if the market suddenly crashed they would no longer have a purpose or a place; the tension between self-loathing and self-respect sometimes kept her up at night, watching the moths fly by her light and cast shadow puppets on the wall.

Jenni got on well with the other divers, a crew of thirty women all dedicated to providing, to the ocean, and to trying to find a way to carry out their work sustainably while still meeting corporate demands. Jenni was the youngest. They would line up at the dock at seven, amid yawns and breakfast, departing in their boat at eight. They'd perched on the back in their wetsuits, like penguins symmetrically mirroring each other, watching the sun continuing its ascent over the horizon. Water was cut up behind them, the boat's motor and body leaving a bloody trail of white. They'd look around at each other, all made uniform in wetsuit and hood, masks on-top of their heads, knowing they had each other's backs as much as they could.

Since her mother's death, there had been only one other diver who had gotten caught in an undertow and banged her head against the reef. Unconscious, and with everyone else invested in their own work, she drowned. Nobody realised she had even disappeared until the roll call that night, and her body did not emerge until three days later. Jenni did not know her all that well, but they had shared soup the day before her death. The second body was experienced even more abstractly than the first. She still felt sadness for the woman, but having had less connection to the woman, didn't even cry. She mourned a person she could never know, the inevitability of connection painful. She mourned for the people she had connected with. She mourned for the person lost. But mostly, she was angry at the system they had been wrapped in. Then the mourning was over and they moved on.

It was a cold morning; her breath tapered out in front of her like a ghost. She rubbed her hands together, careful to put her gloves on. Her boots had always been a little tight, snug as ingrown toenails. The boat had once taken off without her. She'd been too busy trying to get her diving booties on, and had almost slipped off the pier in alarm at seeing the boat pulling away. Today, those boots were safely attached to her feet and the prosthetic fins. A managerial woman was pointing her crab gauge like a gun at the woman next to her in a mock argument. Jenni checked her collection bag, aware there was a slight tear in the mesh. It had not gotten worse, but she still would have to replace it tomorrow. She wore her float cover like a backpack, and could feel her own gauge digging into her shoulder blade.

A DolTHINK tanker was visible further out into the ocean, cleaving through the blue of the sky and white of the morning mist. From this distance, it looked like a moderately large Jenga block floating on the surface, or a turd floating to the top. Just looking at it brought a stink to her nostrils. She picked up the water bottle by her feet, scuffed and bloated from overuse and salt spray, and took a sip. She counted to ten, pointedly not looking towards the horizon. A pity: the gradual dawn light was always beautiful. A dull haze, yellowing like an old page in the sky. Mist would roll in, muting the razed sky. Looking at the ocean was like looking at endless shifting fields, little lines of light mosaicking the waterscape. Clouds dragging up colour, whilst being a thick purple-grey colour themselves. Some mornings, she'd imagine a pier would extend out from the boat to this horizon, but the closer it got the more concealed in the fog it became. She'd imagine walking out to meet the horizon, to meet the sun as it rose, but the closer she felt she was getting to her destination, the more she felt she was walking in place. More mist would depart, in degrees, to reveal more pier. The distance seemed to remain the same. It was relaxing, and the very process of walking, even running, would bring her closer to some truth. Such daydreams revived her.

Janine, a coarse Canadian lady with decaying thirty-year-old skin and aggressively friendly social tact, chuckled and asked if she was okay. "Your expression was hilarious. Like, welcome back to reality, kiddo! How was your trip?"

Jenni just smiled politely and shrugged.

Martina stumbled across the boat, more undone by the thirty bodies than the waves beneath, to sit beside her. The other women accommodated the motion. Martina ruffled her head. "How many years is it today?"

Jenni shrugged again, even though she knew the date and time. Her mother's death was inscribed in scars in her inner wrist, currently hidden beneath the sleeve of her wetsuit

"It's been tough for everyone. And with—what was her name? The new girl? Well, since she died, it's understandable you'd be a bit shaken. Just look after yourself, and don't be as stubborn as your mother when it comes to looking at others for help."

Jenni nodded.

They were getting closer to the drop point, where it was safest to dive and easiest to swim to the areas where crabs were thickest. She patted her head, making sure her hood was secure. Her bootees definitely were; her gloves too. She stood up and patted down her weight belt, tightening it a fraction as it started to slide out of place. Paranoia, really. The weight belt was hardly likely to slide off. There was an art to diving, really. Some of the women preferred to tumble in backwards, sitting on the side of the boat and then rolling off the edge into the water, as this prevented the facemask from being dislodged when entering the water. But Jenni had dreams of jumping straight in, sinking down, down, down, as if she were in an elevator. She never broke from a traditional feet-first drop from the ship, but when she was on her own without the full equipment, she took great pleasure in diving face forward through the waves, levitating under the pull.

Her dives went as follows:

Step one: she would stretch out her fingers and hands, shake out the tension. She'd attach her basket to the pulley rope, the lifeline that went down into the water with her. Then she'd make sure her machete and gauge were safely in hand. These crabs weren't the usual sort, typically two metres tall and four metres wide. Smarter than the average crab, too, they'd learned to avoid holes, nets, and crab traps. It was why the ocean warriors were needed.

Step two: entry. Jenni would sit on the edge, perched and ready to fall into the water's cool embrace. The first few seconds of falling into water was like falling into nothingness, just air whistling through your suit. Then she'd break the surface and the world would go mute and blurred through a green-blue lens, all motion slowing down as if the life teeming beneath was in deep meditation.

Step three: her descent. Falling down, weighted by her belt. It pulled her down without release, ripples and bubbles from her snorkel, a wedding veil trailing above her.

Step four: reach the bottom. Stepping on the green-tinged sand was like walking on the moon, but decorated with rock that cut into, but never penetrating, through her booties. She'd see lobsters retreat under crevasses, sensing the divers, zoning into their frequency shifts and being repelled. Sometimes Jenni would catch one to sell on the side. She had no permit, but there was still a market. The ocean floor was the colour of copper, varying between pure copper and over-oxygenated green. It mosaicked the rocks with vertiginous patterns, disguising the variation in texture and height. Green seagrass shoots stumbled up from the ground, growing between rock patches. The occasional family of sea horses would appear, their tails curled around the grass like organic anchors.

THE ANTHROPOLOGY OF DIVING

The moments between step three and step four was the only time she knew peace. She forgot her mother. She forgot her poverty. She forgot the other divers. It was just her, and an infinite expanse of beautiful blue. It lasted a couple of minutes at the greatest depth. Sometimes less.

The moment that infinity became finite was the most jarring. It broke her with memories of having a job to do.

Most days, she just got to work. The crabs typically lounged among the rocks, snacking on any smaller Earth crabs that happened to crawl passed, or else scuttled on the seafloor. It could be difficult to discern them from their background. Sometimes, they'd camouflage themselves as a rock, curling their feet up underneath them, letting the sand cover their true shape. But over time, Jenni had learned how to spot them with ease. She left those that were too small—she had to laugh at the concept of a crab as tall as her being considered too small for consumption, but she wasn't in charge of regulation. She would get to work cornering the big ones, the ones she was legally allowed to take. Slicing a smaller one would be stupid—these alien crabs could not clot their blood, and she would hate to leave the thing dying where it could not grow or be used. She would hate to end up with the same fate under their claws, left discarded in an alien environment. She used her gauge—flicking it out like a measuring tape—to ensure she didn't make any mistakes, making sure the beast was taller than a metre and seventy centimetres, before retracting the contraption. She could barely hear under the water, but each time she stabbed into one, breaking the carapace open with a practiced slice, she'd imagine their forlorn sigh as their legs crumbled beneath them.

She'd dismember the creature, limb by limb, shoving what she could into the basket a segment at a time. When the basket was full, she'd release it so she didn't have to drag it to the surface. Then it would come down again, attached but detachable from the rope for more harvesting of the corpse.

She aimed for three successful confrontations with a crab a day to maximise the amount of food she harvested without burning out, but sometimes she'd be wounded by a crab who had been able to defend itself—where possible, at the first successful slice she'd retreat and resurface. Resurfacing was another moment of suspension, a life-giving pause. A breath in the water. She'd drag it out for as long as she could. She didn't want to leave, and the pull of the water made her feel it didn't want her to leave, either. Here, hers was a world of silence. Breaking the water—entering back into the world of sound, clambering back onto the boat—was her least favourite moment. The sound of the boat purring, the ceaseless, meaningless chatter of the women made her want to drown. To return to the freedoms of the ocean, and the embrace of her mother.

About the Author:

Brianna Bullen is a Deakin University PhD creative writing candidate writing about memory in science fiction. She has had work published in journals including LiNQ, Aurealis, Voiceworks, Rabbit, Multiverse: An anthology of international science fiction poetry, and Woolf Pack Zine.

She won the 2017 Apollo Bay short story competition and placed second in the 2017 Newcastle Short story competition. Her manuscript was previously a finalist in the 2018 Subbed In Poetry Chapbook competition. In 2018, she was part of Nexus, an Arts Access Victoria collective for artists with mental health recovery lived experience.

PHOENIX PHARMACEUTICALS

Jessica Nelson-Tyers

It was hard to connect the scarred, part-plucked chicken of a bird before me with the mighty phoenix of legend. It was small, for one thing. About the size of a bantam hen. Its gender was one of many unknowns about it—every scan they tried was a mess of noise, and its DNA defied analysis. They weren't going to risk vivisection, thank god. It was their only sample, so they didn't want to lose it. That'd be like gutting the goose that laid the golden eggs.

The bird—we'd been told not to give it a name, even in private—began a fine tremor at the sight of me. I opened three pieces of mint gum and popped them into my mouth, chewing hard to get the fresh flavour going. The wrappers fell like autumn leaves to the concrete floor. Nausea had been a problem for me at first, but Mac suggested chewing gum and it helped, it really helped. It seems crazy now that the bastard thought I could fight off my conscience with the taste of toothpaste. Crazier that it worked.

I ran my hand over the lab tools, slow as a snake in winter. The suspense added to the psychological trauma I had to produce. My fingers touched lightly on a scalpel and a ball-peen hammer before curling round the pliers.

The phoenix had long tail feathers once, bright as sunset and soft as blossom. They made it look like something special, but the pliers took them, and for some reason they never grew back.

I was the one who worked out the most effective way to get the tears flowing. It was the way it responded, like it knew what was going on. It was clever, brainier than a bin chicken or a statue-shitter pigeon. Watching the security cameras and the electric doors. Holding out as long as it could each time, denying us those precious droplets as though it resented us.

So one day, instead of cutting it, I sat down and told it my sob story. How Glenn and I found each other, how we got married and thought we'd be together forever. Then the cancer, eating him alive from inside, chewing his lungs, his throat and his stomach to pieces, seeding its way into his brain.

I told it Glenn was on the verge of death, how I didn't like causing pain, but I didn't want the love of my life to die. How I was being eaten up too, with everything that made me human being devoured. I'd have held myself together a little if I could—I was at work and on video after all—but the more I spoke, the more my nose and eyes dripped, adding fresh marks to my already stained lab coat. When I spotted the tear sliding over the phoenix's beak, I gestured to the lab techs to get over with a pipette and a beaker, quick.

Sara tried to follow my lead. She'd been cured a way back, but she laid it on thick, showing pictures of some random kids, pretending they were hers. Crying because they'd be orphaned. Poor ickle things. The phoenix cocked its head to the side and made a squawk-squawk, like the first two notes of a kookaburra's laugh. It stayed dry the whole morning with Sara wheedling at it, until she grabbed the screws and crushed a toe. It was laughing on the other side of its beak then.

Turns out it could tell when someone was lying, which had all kinds of potential. Pity it couldn't talk.

There's an animal, a sort of bearcat, native to the forests of Southeast Asia. I saw it in a zoo once. Its biggest claim to fame is that it smells like popcorn. It does, too. Its scent, as it paced in its cage, was just like the movies—buttered popcorn with a hint of sweat.

Know what a frightened Phoenix smells of?

Fireworks. Close your eyes and you're in a crowd on a summer evening, watching something dangerous and beautiful. Open them again and you're back in hell, holding the pitchfork.

The reality of medical science meant the first tears were wasted on rabbits. Goddamn rabbits. The pharmacologists cured their cancers (induced, of course), wrote up the studies, then euthanised the poor beasts anyway.

This might have gone on for years, the testing, the waiting—but when Prime Minister Bob Bronner got sick, it all went out the window. He denied it, but he was dying. Every doctor, scientist and snake oil salesman in the country lined up to give their two cents, but the consensus was that nothing could be done. When Phoenix Pharmaceuticals stepped in, it caused an uproar.

One day he was wasting away on national television, clinging onto office despite his jaundiced skin and withered physique. Answering press questions with his usual wit, but slowly and with dead eyes. If he hadn't yet been ousted by his party, it was only because they didn't want to look cruel to the public eye. He was a problem that would go away on its own. The sharks were circling.

Next day, he strode out onto the platform, announced his cure to the world. The miracle had come, the answer to his prayers, in the form of a medical breakthrough from Phoenix Pharmaceuticals. That Friday he took first place in the City to-Surf marathon. No kidding.

PHOENIX PHARMACEUTICALS

Now the only things standing between people and the elixir of life were money and conscience.

Guess which won out?

The big payday for Phoenix Pharmaceuticals came when they found they could dilute a tear to a one-hundredth part and it'd still be effective. There are only so many sick billionaires in the world to milk for all they've got. This revelation opened the cure to the millionaires, plus a few lucky workers who'd do anything for a drop. Anything.

On my own big payday, I drove to work with a flutter that flowed from my heart to my hands. I'd been working in pharmaceutics for three months. It had been a hell of a probation period. Things were getting hairy for Glenn: the doctors said it wouldn't be much longer. His hands were so thin I could see the skeleton underneath. It reminded me how we're all just meat over a frame, and there's nothing to stop us winking out like a dying star.

The company makes a big deal about its philanthropy for its workers. Sara got in early, did alright, but Sammy, he got too sick to work and died before his payday.

That scenario played out in my head, drowning out the yells of the protesters as I drove in. I imagined arriving at the hospital with the cure that night and finding an empty bed.

The razor wire closed me in with the bird. Featherless now. Looked like a cockatoo with beak and feather disease. If I'd been able to name it, I'd have called it Lady Godiva.

It was getting harder to make it cry. How many tears could it possibly have left in it? It had stopped drinking long ago, but they hooked it up with a feeding tube and restrained its head and claws so it wouldn't be able to pull it out. Still, what if they didn't work like us, on hydration and misery alone? What if there's a wellspring in them that can dry up, and once it's gone, it's gone?

That day I brought in my tablet. Trying to ignore the cameras, I took a deep breath to get into the zone. I plastered concern on my face and showed it a video of a sun bear in a bile extraction facility. Got liquid in record time.

Mac called me into his office at closing time. A little amber bottle glittered on his side of the desk. He drew my hand into his own. Cold, smooth and manicured. I hadn't cut my own nails in weeks.

"How is Glenn?" he whispered. Mac almost always spoke in a whisper. Perhaps he was a butler in another life, trained not to raise his voice.

I swallowed. "Not good." My voice cracked, so I stopped speaking. My hands itched to slap him. This man could have cured Glenn months ago if he hadn't wanted leverage over me.

He didn't make a move to pass me the bottle. I'd have snatched it from the table and run if I could.

PHOENIX PHARMACEUTICALS

"I do hope you'll continue with us once he's cured. We need workers with your imagination and finesse." Mac pushed a contract across the table towards me.

My breath came shallower. He was corralling me before I'd even had a chance to say I was leaving. I wouldn't put that cure in jeopardy.

The contract specified a year, strict confidence and a salary in the hundreds of thousands. The bottle glinted.

I signed.

As always, a moron ruined everything. Leon bloody Carter. He made the empire fall. Anyone with a smattering of mythological comprehension knows phoenixes are flammable. This guy was illiterate. Probably not even sick like the rest of the crew—or sick in a different way. A bit too keen to get results, if you know what I mean. Probably practised on puppies as a kid. Anyway, this psychopath had the bright idea to use fire.

The security footage shows him pulling a lighter from his pocket and applying it to the underside of the phoenix's claw. He was probably expecting to hear it squawk, get the tears coming really thick and fast. Instead the flame licked up the bird's leg like a wick. You can see Carter jump back, for all the good it did him. The video cuts to static there. It delighted news corporations around the world before the end of the day.

The aftermath showed the bird had detonated like a miniature nuke, leaving blast shadows on the walls where the techs had been standing. Those poor saps were left as charred husks, and as far as I know nobody ever found what was left of Leon.

In stories, the phoenix is reborn from the ashes, but although they left the room intact for weeks (cremated staff included), the legends proved wrong.

That was it. A relief, really, except for the thought of all the people who'd never get their cure. Glenn had been given the all-clear a month prior, so I was looking for an out. The redundancy package was generous enough to allow me some time off—maybe six months or a year to relax with Glenn, drinking home-made martinis on the back porch, finally getting the veggie garden under control.

I won't say I never had trouble sleeping. Sometimes when I hit the hay too early, I saw blood and feathers and tears. Other times I thought too much about the stories I told the phoenix, and how they were all true, and this world is a hellish place. Then Glenn would hop into bed and curl up around me, and that was all the world I needed, right there.

The round lump on the scan made me scream like a rabbit caught in a trap. It was a mass the size of a golf ball, nestled deep in the folds and crevasses of Glenn's brain.

"It's inoperable," the GP murmured. She explained they'd have to cut through too much to reach it. There were some anomalies on the scan and she'd arrange for a specialist, but given Glenn's history there was a high likelihood that it was a return of the cancer. It had caused the onset of his seizures and other symptoms, of course. As the doctor outlined Glenn's options, I considered smashing her computer from her desk, ripping her framed degrees and kid's paintings from the wall. In the end I just sat there, tearing a pamphlet to bits.

He sagged onto me in our car afterwards. I stroked my hands through his hair again and again. The smell of car fresheners still brings me back there. Fresh with an undertone of death, like a corpse in a pine forest.

"How could this happen?" Glenn whispered into my shoulder. "Phoenix tears are meant to cure everything. We were meant to grow old together."

It was clear what had happened. Mac, that sonovabitch. He must've diluted it too much, till it was only an interim cure, as shitful and as weak as he was.

That night I dreamed of work. I dreamed of cutting and twisting. I dreamed that even tears didn't stop me. I dreamed of using the pliers to yank out teeth, and woke when Mac drowned in his own blood.

We both rose with the sun and snapped on the TV for a reprieve from our own thoughts. The whirr of the coffee machine made things feel normal. Maybe it would wake us enough to emerge from our nightmare.

Glenn gestured to the telly. Prime Minister Bronner, smiling and slick, was the centre of a crowd of workers who should have known better, really. He was wearing a hard hat and a fluro vest, looking like a kid in dress-ups.

"How come he gets the happy ending?" asked Glenn. "He breezes through life, screws the country, and gets to cheat death, too."

What could I say?

We stared at Bronner, who sold his sympathy for the cause, his empathy for hard-up workers with a slick car-dealer's demeanour. He faltered mid-speech and lost his croc's grin. He tore off his vest and the work shirt underneath. An aide leaned in close to him to whisper, probably scoping out what the issue was—a spider in his shirt, perhaps? He leapt away as smoke and blood blossomed from Bronner's abdomen, just below the ribs. Bronner sagged to the ground like a scarecrow off its stick.

I set down my coffee and turned up the volume.

The camera jolted then tracked back to the action. There were screams about snipers and bombs; workers and reporters running for cover. Then movement at Bronner's body.

A beak poked through the open wound, followed by a head and smoking wings. The chick flopped onto the ground, feathers fully formed, bloody and bright as a fiery dawn. It sped across the grass, flapping its wings and jumping like a chicken on the run. It left a trail of smouldering entrails as it went.

It struggled to make it off the ground at first, but it launched itself like a drunk chook and somehow made it to the top of a nearby lamppost, where it sat carolling. It sounded like a cross between a magpie and an angel. All I could think was that the phoenix I knew never made those sounds.

A cop took potshots at the thing, but it flew, and hey—who knows—maybe it made it.

Glenn realised what it meant first. His coffee mug smashed all over the floor as he dropped it to claw at his head. I didn't know what he was on about until he started screaming.

"It's not a tumour. It's not a tumour, it's an egg. Get it out of me! Get it out!"

About the Author:

Jessica Nelson-Tyers has previously had stories published in magazines and anthologies ranging from children's fiction to the darkest horror. She tries not to get confused about where she is submitting. Jessica has a Graduate Diploma in Professional Writing and is part of the Andromeda Spaceways Publishing team. She lives with her family on a bush property on the coast, which provides her with all kinds of weird inspiration. You can find her at jessicanelsontyers.com or follow her tweets @JessNelsonTyers.

THE BINDI

Emily Siggs

The sweet smell of heather. The running of water over jagged
rocks. Fish with shiny, silver bodies slipping through the current.
The piercing cries of a drowning woman.

Nadia was used to it. The river was dangerous, and the people
of the land understood that. But they did not understand the ways
in which it was dangerous. The strong current. Hidden rocks and
submerged logs. Heather hiding where the bank begins and ends.
The river knows your secrets.

This would be the third this month. She paddled towards the
cries, the splash of her oars drowned out by the tumble of water.
The Bindi was thin but long, and twisted through the current like
an eel. The hull was scratched and weatherworn, with endless
layers of wax painted over it to prevent leaks. It was an extension
of her body, and Nadia easily guided her canoe around the rocks.

"I'm coming!" If they could hear her over the rush of the water, it would be another challenge entirely to comprehend her strange, lilting accent. "Hold onto the bank!"

There she was—a village girl, no doubt, her water-pot already washed downstream as the many layers of her dress, apron and petticoat dragged her down. Splash. Splosh. The familiar slow beat of human hands resisting the water. The white crinoline bloomed and turned in the rapids like a giant jellyfish. Why these humans wore such things, Nadia was not sure. Some humans were more acclimatised to the river and wore shorter, lighter garments. They lived alongside her, knew of her, but spoke of her not: only the women around the fire at night would tell the children how to respect the river, and that the river kept your secrets.

The girl saw Nadia and splashed more, attempting to reach the canoe. Her auburn hair, which had been tied in a simple but elegant bun, was sopping wet and coming loose. Her thick black shoes must have been pulling her down like iron strapped to her feet. "Help! Help!"

Then she went under. The current swept her further towards the jagged rocks. She surfaced again, gasped for air, and went back to screaming.

Nadia had never met another like herself, save one: her sister, Nerual. While Nadia was of fresh water, Nerual dwelled in the sea-salty ocean. She wore an eye patch like the human sailors and commandeered a ship that had been wrecked on the rocks. Nerual had fixed it with her own hands and, instead of humans, she rescued the fish, sharks, dolphins and other Strange Folk who couldn't swim, choking in fishing nets or with harpoons lodged in their tails, taking them aboard her ship and nursing them back to health in the dark, flooded hold.

Nadia maneuvered the Bindi near the girl and extended a webbed hand. "Here!"

The girl grabbed uselessly and missed; Nadia leaned further. They were always too busy drowning to notice her long, greasy black hair, the webbed skin of her fingers or the brilliant green hue of her eyes, let alone the gills on her neck.

The girl tried again, but the current was too strong. Her strength was gone, and as she sunk beneath the surface, took a breathful of water.

Nadia jumped from the Bindi, and the cold, clear water drew her in and hugged her like it never wanted to let go. She lunged, catching the girl around her apron-tied waist. She was heavy. Humans were always heavy. Nadia's heart quickened. This current was much stronger than she'd thought.

Nadia pulled her and swum against the current. Every second the girl let more water into her lungs, and every second they were swept closer to the rocks. The river was Nadia's mother, but it would still tear her to shreds against them.

The water was murky with silt the rapids ripped up from the riverbed. Nadia closed her gills to shut it out, and now she too could not breathe. Her eyes were also being peppered with silt. Her vision was failing. How close were the rocks?

Nadia felt for the girl's shoes and ripped them off, the current dragging them away. She was perhaps a little lighter, but not enough. Still feeling blindly and swimming as hard as she could, Nadia took the little obsidian knife from her belt and cut the girl's apron free. No. Still too heavy! Nadia cut the girl free from her dress, slicing layers of the skirt away where they were ripped to shreds on the rocks. It was not enough. Without further sacrifice, this current would drown them both. Nadia sawed at the girl's long auburn hair where it was tied and cut it short, the rest of her lengths taken by the river who would keep them forever.

She was finally light enough: perhaps one hair's weight between saveable and lost to the rocks. That is, if Nadia had enough oxygen left to take her to the surface. Her lungs burned, full of water and silt, as she dragged the girl towards the sunlight.

With one last pull, Nadia broke the surface and gasped for air, shoving her knife back in her belt, before towing the girl to the bank. Thin arms trembling, she pulled the girl into the heather and rolled her over. Her eyes were closed, face tinged with blue, body as white as the haphazard slices of ripped petticoat that still stuck to her here and there. Nadia took her face in her hands and breathed life back into her, until her lips and cheeks began to regain the rose-blush of life.

By the time the girl opened her eyes, Nadia was already making her way towards the sea. It was always better not to be there when they woke, so villagers didn't come looking with fire torches. So they always explained the shadowy images of the green-skinned maiden who saved them as imaginings of their drowning brains. She wondered if the girl would remember anything when she woke, naked and soaked in the heather, hair cut short. Whether she would blame the fey for her shame, say they stole her hair, or say nothing, keeping it in her heart like a treasure. She wondered whether the touch of her lips, her breath, would make the girl see strange dancing lights in the woods and drink water like a fish. She wondered whether Nerual would laugh and say, 'why do you save them, when they never learn?' She wondered if the river would wash up the dress on the shore of the forest humans, who would push it back in tenderly and murmur, "this is the river's secret".

About the Author:

Emily Siggs is a writer, editor and poet with a propensity for the delightfully bizarre. She wrote this story for her mermaid-loving, Cancer-sign sister, Lauren. She won the youth section of the 2016 Patron's Prize for Poets with 'Tuesday Mornings', *and in 2020, conducted a project for the Centre for Stories on dancers from many cultures, Australian Aishwaryas. She is currently working on an experimental dark fantasy novella,* 'Nefelibata'. *Her Instagram handle is emilyexploresspace.*

KARKINOS

Nikky Lee

Water presses cool against my face. Below, the seabed is quiet; a sweet stillness broken by the faint 'click-click' of parrotfish biting away chunks of coral. I drag in a lungful of air and bubbles hiss up from my tank. God, I love this place—I should have come back sooner.

With a kick I surge forward, heading for the wreck on my underwater horizon. It's even more overgrown with coral than I remember. Fish dart in and out of portholes and between rigging laden with seagrass. The visibility is superb. Thirty meters at least. I haven't seen it like this since . . .

Since Mary.

We never found out what happened. Not for sure. She went out for a snorkel one day—not far, she said, just off the beach—and never came back. Then noon trickled into evening and I called the police. Searched everywhere. Other bays, the reef, the wreck— no sign. Hit by a boat, some said. Taken by a shark, said others.

And my Mary was gone. Cut from my life clean as a doll cut from paper, with nothing but a Mary-shaped hole left behind. I scoured that beach for five years, hoping against hope I would find some clue, a trace, an answer, anything. I looked for her in the faces of strangers every trip into town. Nothing.

Keegan talked me into the funeral. *"You've got to move on Dad."*

Shortly after, at Keegan's insistence, I picked up my shattered pieces, closed the door on our family home of forty years and left for Broome.

I hadn't been back since. Not in eight years.

A school of angelfish scatter as I glide down to investigate a table coral. Its colour is vivid, orange and pink. I hang there, suspended, feeling the faint pull of the current. *What would it be like,* I wonder, *to simply float away?* To forget the aches and pains of the world above and drift?

A dart of movement draws me back to the wreck. With a flick of fins and a scooping of hands, I turn, an ungainly whale of neoprene and air tank. It's a crab; nestled down in the broken hold. Its blue carapace glints through the weed and coral fingers, and I drop closer and closer again, hoping for a better look. Its shell is at least the width of my splayed hand. Perhaps bigger. A good size. *A good supper.* I snatch at it. My gloved hand gives a faint tremble before my fingers clamp around the crab's abdomen and pull it from its cranny. Its legs kick, pincers writhe, antennae whirl. I drop it inside my dive net.

It stares up at me, black eye stalks forlorn through its prison net. My stomach gives the tiniest of guilty twists. Circle of life, buddy.

Let it go. A memory of Mary visits me. It's the height of summer and I'm fishing off the town jetty; she's ridden her pushbike up to see what I've caught. She doesn't know me then, not really. But she frowns when she peers into my bucket and sees the crab I've netted from the muddy shallows.

"Let it go," she says at once.

I stare at this girl—almost a woman, but not quite—who tries to tell me what to do with my catch.

"No way," I say. *"That's dinner."*

She wrinkles her nose. *"It's mean."* Her eyes settle on me and glint with a hint of mischief I'll come to know well. *"And . . ."*

"And what?"

The corners of her mouth tick up, like she's suddenly letting me in on a secret. She leans in. *"And I don't much fancy crab for dinner."*

I blink, astonished, then grin and hold out my hand. *"Name's Roy, Roy Quin. Pick you up at seven?"*

Like that, we met. Over a crab. Fifty years married we would have been, come tomorrow. When she didn't come back that day, when she must have inevitably sunk to the seafloor, the crustaceans probably picked her corpse—

I wrench my mind away, bubbles belching from my regulator as my heart flips in my chest. Don't think it. Not of her . . . not like that. My eyes burn behind my mask. I check my dive gauge. Half a tank left, but my enthusiasm has waned. It's been enough for this old man. I turn to go.

A metallic gleam from the hole I pulled the crab from catches my eye. I stop, squint and push some weed away, revealing a crusted—I pause, not quite able to believe it—handle? I feel my fingers further into the hole, trying to discern whatever it is that's lodged inside. Despite the algae and barnacles, its shape is unmistakably rectangular. I dig my fingers around it, brace my fins against the bones of the deck and pull.

The crab in my dive net kicks and twitches, waves its pincers like angry fists.

A box slides out the hole—covered in rust and baby coral. I stare, recognising what it is at once.

A safe.

The safe is heavy and I'm puffing by the time I haul it along the beach, up the sand track, and place it on the rickety table in the living room. Water puddles across the dry wood, bringing the smell of brine and seaweed with it. I eye the lock, or what's left of it: a barnacled knot of metal and cemented sand. One decisive blow with a hammer could snap it clean off, but I don't have anything like that here. I left it all with Keegan back in Broome. If

I call him now, I'll get a lecture about diving alone. He'd not been keen on me moving back here as it was.

"Are you sure, Dad?" he'd asked, hazel eyes earnest like Mary's. *"It's a long way from anywhere. And with your health . . ."*

I'd told him, in no uncertain terms, that that was the point. *"I'm dying. Nothing you or me or the doctors can do about it. I'm doing this while I can."*

My son had sighed, looked like he'd wanted to say more, until Zoe had run into the hallway, begging her father to see the model train set she'd assembled. With a meaningful glance as he was pulled away, he'd said: *"I'll check up on you every other week. Call if you need anything. And take your pills."*

I turn the safe around on the table, ignoring how the barnacles scrape gouges into the wood. The safe is small, not more than a box really, and barely a hand deep. I rummage through the kitchen drawers, my shaky hands scattering the cutlery until I finally catch a butter knife. Back at the table, I wedge it through the lock's arched shackle and twist. The pressure builds, and the disease trembles my hands. I growl and adjust my grip, leaning my weight on the knife. The silverware bends instead. And just when I think it is going to fold in two, the clasp of the lock snaps. With a ping, sand and flakes of rust scatter across the table.

"Ha!" I bark in triumph and reach for the lid. And stop.

A scratching, clicking sound comes from the kitchen.

Frowning, I leave the safe untouched and go to investigate.

It's the crab. Crawling across the floor, dragging my dive bag with it. The critter has pulled itself up and out of the kitchen sink and made a break across the tiles. Its plate-sized shell gleams a stormy blue in the evening light. The eye stalks swivel on me; pincers snap up.

And it charges.

Yes, *charges*. Crab-runs sideways at me it does, pincers raised, legs skittering over the tiles. I step out of its way. I'm barefoot; I don't fancy one of those pincers around my toes.

The crab follows. Still coming for me.

"What in the—" I backpedal, a familiar stiffness tinged with pain turns my gait awkward and ungainly, like my legs don't belong to me anymore.

Still the crab comes.

I lunge for the sagging sofa, near falling onto it, and with effort, heave my feet up after me.

The crab stops. Its antennae twitch, eye stalks shift from me to the dripping safe on the table. And there it stays. Watching.

Slowly, I uncoil on the sofa, lower one foot on the floor, then the other, and wait. The critter doesn't move.

Get ahold of yourself Roy, it's just a crab.

With a groan, I haul myself onto my feet. My muscles spasm with the effort. I miss the water already, the weightlessness of it, the freedom from my shaking. How easy it is to move again.

I approach the crab, thinking to scoop up the end of the dive net and return it to the sink, but as I come close, its pincers rise, claws open. I take one step towards the creature and it thrusts its pincers out, warding me off. When I try to grab the dive net, it scuttles around and lunges for my hand. I snatch my fingers back, cursing. Little cretin nearly got me.

I back up and the crab settles, squatting into itself like an irate spider.

"Think you've won, eh?"

The crab, for its part, jerks its antennae like it's flipping me the bird.

I grind my teeth and think of the bucket under the laundry sink. How I might thump it down over the wily crustacean and jostle it back into my sink, and then into a pot.

When I do thump said bucket over the crab, it goes ballistic. Its legs scrabble, sounding like a rat under the floorboards. It claws bang against its plastic prison, and the bucket skitters across the floor as it tries to free itself. I heft a dusty, spine-split Macquarie dictionary with both hands from the bookshelf. My muscles quiver as I carry it tight against my chest, then drop it on top of the bucket to hold it down.

With a sigh, I shuffle to the table where I'd left the safe. I hold my breath as my hands clench the lid—a strong grip to stop the tremors—and push it up. It opens soundlessly. Not so much as a squeak. I blink. I'd expected a shrieking of rusted hinges, a groan of metal, but the lid swings open like it's freshly oiled. Strange.

Thunk, thunk, thunk. The crab bashes its bucket.

I look inside the safe.

105

I don't know what I was expecting. A few corroded coins, perhaps a quill and inkpot, remnants of a journal, though the pages would have disintegrated years ago; maybe a pocket watch.

Thunk, thunk, thunk, goes the crab.

I stare. Hot and cold flush through me. My belly curdles.

It's a heart.

It's not a human heart. Too big. Far, *far* too big. Four of my fists in size at least. And it's metal. Cogs and gears and springs are enclosed behind a glass carapace. Brass funnels curl out of its top and side: the aorta and main arteries. A clock face lies over one ventricle—strange and impossibly small symbols are carved where the numbers should be, each one a series of dots and lines. Twelve in all. The clock itself has two hands: one is normal looking, the other has a tiny orb at its end painted half black, half white.

But that's not the clincher.

The clincher is that *it's moving.*

Deep within the heart, the fine gears slowly turn. It takes a long minute for me to be sure, but yes, there it goes, a tooth in the largest gear clicks over.

A breath shudders out of me. "Incredible." How has such a thing survived the sea? Waterproof. It must be. New too, surely. There's no tarnish of age. But what about the state of the safe? All appearances suggest it has been underwater for tens of years, if not hundreds.

With tentative hands, I lift the heart out of the safe. It's heavy. I tighten my grip on it, feeling the tell-tale quiver in my fingers. The brass and glass surface slides in my grip. It's still wet. Slippery too.

And *warm.*

I swallow.

Then the heart beats. The metal doesn't shift, not like a heart of flesh might, but *something* shivers through my hands, up my arms.

I nearly drop it on the table.

That's when I see the reverse side. Another clock face. Only this one has various shaded circles depicted on it; its single hand pointed at a waxing circle, almost full. *It's the moon.*

Thunk, thunk, thunk. I jump as the crab starts up its banging again. Stronger than before. The bucket scrapes across the floor, gaining a few centimetres. I consider my find on the table a moment longer, then go out back to retrieve my dive gloves. They're still wet, but I pull them on and head into the lounge. The bucket has moved another half metre.

With a sigh, I lift off the dictionary, remove the bucket and scoop the crab up in the dive net. I take it outside and sit on the back deck to untangle it. It is tedious work; the crab's pincers chomp down on my gloved fingers and don't let go until I pry its claws apart. I curse. Several times. The thing's like a bloody limpet. And every time I loosen a claw, its antenna thrash furiously. I can almost imagine it swearing at me.

At last I get it free. I pull myself up on the handrail and shuffle across the yard, past the leaning picket fence and along the sandtrack through the dunes.

"You're in luck today, crab." I tell it as I set it down on the beach. "Any other time and I'd have eaten you."

I release the crustacean. But instead of scuttling off, it stands there. Pincers lax and open. Almost as if I've surprised it. I roll my eyes at the thought. *It's a crab, for Pete's sake.* I flick a bit of sand at it with my toes.

"Go on, off you go. If you're so keen to live, go get on with it."

When it doesn't move, I shrug, turn and creak back over the dune. A smile crooks my lips as I walk.

That was for you, Mary.

Plink, plink.

I wake to the sound of coins clinking together. Coins? I'm imagining it, surely. Half asleep and with the stiffness holding my limbs to ransom, I open my eyes and listen.

Plink, plink, it comes again. And when I strain my ears: rustling, scratching, clicking. I stare into the dark, my stomach shrivelling into a gristly knot. The darkness isn't the still, quiet dark I've always known. It's moving; shadows within shadow shifting and rolling, and my mind fills with the thought of bugs carpeting the floor.

I claw my body up, levering myself on the bedside table. My muscles shudder—they're always particularly bad first thing in the morning before I take my medicine; like Tin Man left out in the rain. Fingers find the nightstand lamp, tap it on. Light flares.

And my floor moves. Blues, reds, browns and oranges, scuttle away from the lamp. The yell rises in my throat and gets lodged there. A hacking, spluttering cough comes out instead.

Crabs. Hundreds of them. Different shapes, sizes, species: there, a mud crab found in the local estuary, and there, a golden ghost crab, and over there a lopsided fiddler.

Plink, plink. I round on the sound coming from the foot of the bed. A mound of metal sits at my feet, covered in algae and dripping a puddle into my sheet. As I gape, a hermit crab, no bigger than my palm, crawls over the foot of the bed and drops a gold coin onto the pile. Despite the coin's green corroded tint, I spot the unmistakable markings of an Australian dollar.

"Consider this payment," a small voice rises from my nightstand.

I spin, heart buoying up my chest and into my throat.

There's a crab on my nightstand. A familiar crab. The very one I'd set loose on the beach some hours ago now, I'm sure of it. Big and blue and . . .

I hesitate, suddenly not trusting my eyes.

. . . Not a crab?

I mean, it's a crab, but the longer I look, the less crab-like it becomes. It stands erect on three sets of legs, one of which taps as if its patience is thinning. The next pair are folded, like a set of arms, and above that thrust its claws, gesticulating to get my attention.

"Yes, down here. Good, you can hear me properly. At last."

Gobsmacked, I lean in. The eyestalks on its head change, looking more and more like an odd armoured helm. Its antennae and mouth shift too, until a strange humanoid face stares back at me; antennae like a living beard on its chin.

"What . . . what . . . is—are . . ?"

The crab-man gives something of a little sigh, his shell shrugging. "I am Guardian Tasi, and we—" he waves his claws out to the room— "are karkinoi."

My gaze follows Tasi's claws and as it does, the crabs before me change too. Each one turns into tiny humanoids with armoured bodies and antennae on their chins.

I'm hallucinating. That's it. Only explanation. I flop onto my pillow, rub my face, check the nightstand again.

He's still there.

Fuck. All right, think. First thing, call Keegan. Tell him I've gone crackers, full kitchen sink nuts. Though, truth be told, I'd always thought my independence would be claimed by disease, not insanity. The thought boils inside me. I feel cheated. This was supposed to be my last hurrah. Sunset years while I could still have them. And I'd barely been here a week.

"You're not crazy. You folk always seem to think that. Now, to business." Tasi snaps his pincers. "We wish to trade."

110

"Trade?"

"Yes, we have brought you gold and coins given to the sea. A small fortune, yes? We wish to trade it for the heart."

"The heart?" The clockwork heart on my lounge table flashes into my head. *That* heart? But what could these probably-just-my-imagination karkinoi crab folk want with it? "Why?" I blurt.

"A sea witch trusted it to our keeping long ago. It was our— *my*—duty to guard it." He glares at the edge of the nightstand, not meeting my eye. "To keep it safe."

Despite the scene of crabs in my bedroom, I lift an eyebrow. "You didn't do a very good job of it, if you don't mind me saying."

Tasi's leg stamps hard on the nightstand. The mottled blue of his shell darkens. "I *do* mind, but what's done is done."

Seems I hit a nerve.

Tasi folds his claws. "Landfolk usually don't see us or our treasures at all. But somehow you did. You took it and bested me. So now I am here to trade for it."

I blink at the karkinoi, thinking of how the crab had bashed at the bucket when I'd opened the safe. How it had thrashed and bit when I'd freed it from the dive net. He was right, I *had* bested him. But if I were to set my chin on the nightstand, he'd barely come up to my brow. Hardly something to be proud of. To him I am giant; monstrous; a Goliath in the extreme. And still he stands there, annoyed, granted, but ready to barter. Got to admire the courage of the fellow. To think I'd nearly put him in a pot. But something Tasi said comes back to me and I frown.

"You said I saw you, but I didn't. Until tonight you looked . . ." I hesitate, wondering if saying 'crab' might be construed as derogatory, the same way 'monkey' might to a human. "Not like you do now," I amend.

"You saw the lockbox, and Tasi in his guise. Before you touched the heart that is," a new voice wheezes from my elbow. I start and look down. The hermit crab, the same one that'd dropped its coin at the foot of my bed, has scuttled up without my noticing. It's barely a third the size of Tasi as it stands on its back pairs of legs. Its features are finer still; the shell on its back reminding me of a giant snail's. But when I look closer, there's markings—tiny writing—all over the shell.

"If I were to guess, I'd say you were partially sighted," the hermit crab says and scratches one claw to its scraggly antennae-beard as if thinking. "It is rare among landfolk, but not unheard of."

Its voice is rasping and higher pitched, like it might be an old female hen. But it's a guess at best. I'm hardly the expert.

"Lorekeeper Wehi." Tasi acknowledges the newcomer with a bob of a claw. Wehi returns the greeting.

"But I've never seen you before or the safe," I point out. "And I've dived that wreck hundreds of times."

Wehi shifts, her shell cocks to one side. "Mmm, the gift comes and goes, it's said. Most common in children. And sometimes the elderly when . . ." she trails off, and I sense hesitation; something in the way all her legs suddenly still. "Are you ill, man of land?"

112

The weirdness of it clicks together into an odd logic and I sigh. "Call me Roy, and yes."

"Is it terminal?"

I shift in my sheets. It's not something I like to dwell too much on. "Yes. But with any luck, not for several years."

Wehi scratches her antennae again. "Then that explains it."

Tasi's leg taps twice on the nightstand, clearly impatient. "As curious as this is, Lorekeeper Wehi, Roy of Land, I would ask we stick to the topic at hand: the trade." Tasi motions a pincer to the mound of coins. "Are you willing to accept this in exchange for the heart?"

I wave his words off. "I have no use for gold. I have everything I need here. And in a few years it won't matter at all. If the heart is so important, please, have it."

Tasi and Wehi stare at me aghast.

"We cannot do that," Tasi says. "There must be a trade, it is our law."

"It is our way," Wehi adds.

"I can't just give you the heart back?"

"No, you won the heart. Tasi must either best you to win it back or make a trade. And frankly, his chances aren't high at winning—"

Tasi stiffens, his tapping leg stamping hard on my nightstand.

"We karkinoi are not fighters, we rely on stealth and remaining hidden," Wehi explains.

My back aches, but I ease myself up and Wehi scrambles further down the bed as I swing my feet to the floor. "What if I, say, happen to leave the heart on the beach for you? Conveniently lose track of its whereabouts?"

Tasi's claws shoot up, pincers opening wide like he's ready to charge at me. His mottled carapace darkens. "I would *never* stoop to such dishonest—"

"Forget I mentioned it," I say quickly.

"Tasi must trade. Anything else and he forfeits our claim to it." Wehi climbs back over the sheets, stopping a hand's breadth short of my thigh. I glance over at the pile of sea-crusted coins. What harm could it do really? I could send them back to Keegan, perhaps he'd find them worth something.

"Then I suppose I accept your coins."

Tasi throws his claws in the air again. "Should have said it the first time!" His snaps his pincers shut, evidently exasperated. He paces back and forth on the nightstand, muttering something too quiet for these old ears to hear.

"Is there a problem?" I ask Wehi.

The hermit crab's shell rises and falls, as if she has heaved a great sigh. "You have already refused his first offering, now he must find something of greater value. It is . . ."

"Your way," I guess, and now it's my turn to sigh. "Look, there really is nothing I want or need—"

At that, Tasi makes an odd sort of squeaking cry, and his pacing turns frantic. Wehi and I watch him scuttle back and forth on the nightstand. Any second now, I swear he'll wring his claws together.

"Hold on, I'm not finished." I lift a hand to placate him. Tasi's pacing slows, but only a little. "Seeing you, *learning* the karkinoi exist is a gift in itself." And it's true. If only Mary could be here to see them. She would have loved this, not scream and nearly wet herself like I had. She'd always been the more adventurous of the two of us. A familiar ache spreads across my chest. I swallow it down.

"Sadly, a gift is not the same as a trade." Wehi says.

Damn. "All right, what if . . ." I begin, thinking quick. "Would you teach me about the karkinoi and the heart in exchange for it?" I am nothing if not curious.

A quiet takes hold of the room. Tasi stops pacing. Beside me, Wehi falls silent, her antennae-beard still.

"That is a big request," Wehi says.

"It's beyond my rank to authorise," Tasi adds.

"Oh." I chew the inside of my cheek, thinking.

"But I will take you to someone who can." Tasi adds, brightening—if light blue quickening through his carapace is anything to go by. "Yes, this will do." He bobs his claws—some sort of affirmative gesture I'm realising—and scurries down the electrical cord of my nightlight.

A faint tug on my pyjamas turns my attention down again. Wehi has a pincer clamped around the leg of my pyjama bottoms.

"If you'd be so kind, could you return me to your floor, Roy of Land? Not all of us are as spry as Guardian Tasi."

I oblige and scoop her up, my quivering muscles jolting her about on my palm until I cup my other hand over her and deposit her to the floor. When I stand straight, the rest of the crab entourage scuttle into the corners of the room. They are right to fear, I suppose. Humans eat crabs all the time. Catch them by the pot-load. My stomach twists. *I* had eaten my fair share of crabs over the years. Had some of them been karkinoi? But not many humans could see them, right? Mary's words to me all those years ago come back again. Strangely insistent.

Let it go.

A ludicrous, insane thought crosses my mind. *Had she known?*

The sight of Tasi dancing back and forth on the floor pulls me back to the present. "Come, come, Roy of Land."

I frown. "Just Roy is fine. Where are we going?"

"Why, to see Karkinos, of course, the Crab Queen."

"Are you sure I won't drown?" I ask, standing on the beach with the waves lapping my ankles. The sky overhead is the dim purple of pre-dawn.

"Lorekeeper Wehi's charm will protect you," Tasi says, his voice gargling as the water washes over him, turning his blue body into a faint blob of shadow under the whitewash.

I examine the symbols the hermit crab has scratched on my chest, between the curling white hairs. They looked little more than a bunch of squiggles. She'd tried to do it on my hands, but the persistent shake of my muscles had ended that before she'd even started. I hold my fingers up in the moonlight, the shake is noticeable to the naked eye. Today would be a bad episode. I should go back home, rest, take my medicine and sleep the worst of it off.

But the wave washes back out and Tasi scuttles forward, beckoning me.

And I follow, clenching the safe containing the heart to my chest.

The water is oddly warm. Not too hot or cold. A comfortable temperature. A shiver prickles through me. Is it Wehi's charm that's doing this?

"Good, breathe normally," Wehi instructs from my shoulder as I wade in up to my chest. The water stings the fresh cuts of her spell in my skin. Definitely not dreaming. I'm unsure if the thought is comforting or terrifying. The safe weighs me down, anchoring my feet to the seafloor as the water reaches my chin. I lift my head to keep my mouth and nose above the surface, suck in a breath—

"No, breath normally." Pain fires through my earlobe. Wehi's pincer. I yelp, my footing slips, a wave buffets my face, and before I can think I suck *in*. And the water feels light, warm in my throat. It slips into my lungs, effortless, and then it rises again, exhaling

117

through my nose. I blink. The world below is as sharp and clear as the world above.

"Incredible," I whisper, then frown. I sound not quite normal. My voice is deeper and less husky than it is on land.

A small chuckle from my ear, and the pressure on my earlobe releases. Wehi drops from my shoulder and swims for the sandy bottom to wait beside Tasi.

"Come," Tasi beckons. His voice is deeper underwater, more resonant. He curls a leg at me, encouraging, and I catch a gleam of runes there. More karkinoi magic. But before I can wonder what it does, the answer becomes clear. Tasi shoots off across the sea floor. In a heartbeat, he's a good pool length ahead.

"Wha—but—I," I stutter. There's no way I can keep up with that.

"Swim like normal," Wehi advises. "My charm will do the rest." Her voice too has dropped in pitch. If I close my eyes, I can almost feel it wash over my skin.

I tuck the safe under one arm, and kick off the bottom, doing an awkward half breaststroke as I kick my legs. The water rushes past. In half a dozen strokes I've caught up with Tasi. Unbelievable. A tapping of tiny legs follows us, like a cascade of marbles hitting stone. I check behind me, and a wave of crabs flows over the rocks, hundreds of bodies streaking across the seabed.

"Come, come." Tasi waves me on. "I've sent a messenger ahead, Karkinos is waiting."

The seabed drops away, turning to rocks and coral and patches of seagrass. But there's no time for sightseeing. Faster we move, the seafloor formations turning into a blur.

Bit by bit, the number of crabs with us drop away. When I ask Tasi about it, he shrugs one claw.

"They're going home, of course," he says. "We live all over."

"All over where? The reef?"

"Of course."

"This Karkinos you're taking me to, she rules the karkinoi of your reef?"

"No, Wehi is the leader of our colony. Karkinos rules all karkinoi."

"*All* karkinoi? Everywhere?"

"In all oceans, yes," Tasi says simply, as if such a thing is obvious.

I slow my swimming. Where in the world were they taking me then? The thought of going for hours, possibly even days chills my limbs. "How long will it take us to reach her?"

"Not long now, she is on the other side of the reef," Tasi says.

"The Crab Queen lives on *this* reef?" I ask, incredulous. Here, of all places? I might be a gullible old man jetting across a reef on crab magic, but that seems farfetched—too coincidental— even to me.

"Karkinos has paths to every colony," Wehi says from behind and sensing my confusion adds, "you'll see soon, Roy of Land."

And I do. We round a coral atoll and there's a cave burrowed into one side of the underwater island. I gape. The mouth is dark and wide enough for three people to swim abreast through the opening. All those years with Mary diving this reef. How did I not know this was here?

I swing back to ask Wehi, only to catch the smug little smile of Tasi's miniature face. Oh, right, karkinoi magic. Of course.

Tasi puffs himself up, rising onto his back legs as he lifts his claws. "Roy of Land, be sure to show respect. Karkinos rule is absolute here. She made us and can unmake us just as easily." He taps a pincer on his chest. "Wehi's charms keep you alive here, but they can be undone. Remember that."

Karkinos *made* them? Wait, does that mean all karkinoi are her offspring? My mind spins at the thought. Better mind my Ps and Qs then. I swallow, the warm water around me suddenly stifling.

"I will guide you." Wehi's voice sounds in my ear as the prick of legs settles on my shoulder. "Follow Tasi."

I obey.

The tunnel is not overly long, but it is dark. It's all I can do to follow Tasi's blue shell. We round a bend and a pool of light appears high above us. It shimmers like light reflecting on the sea on a sunny day. I frown. That can't be right; we should be deep in the middle of the atoll by now. As we near, the light shifts and moves like shadows moving across a mirror—or behind it. A prickle runs down my legs.

"Go on," Wehi urges.

I take a watery breath and push through the pool.

Air meets me on the other side. I cough, exhale, water gushing from my nose. My fingers find sand and I heave myself out, dragging the dripping safe with me, and stare.

I'm in a clearing. Tropical palms dot the sand. Humid air laps my skin. Overhead, a full moon sheds sliver light on the scene. My mouth drops. There are pools everywhere! Hundreds of them. A scuttle to my left and a crab—legs as long as I am tall, its body the size of my head—drops into an obsidian-black pool with a 'plunk' like a stone into a well.

"Come," Tasi calls from my feet. "Watch your step."

Another crab emerges from a muddy pool to my right. Stops, stares at me, then scurries away.

"They're portholes," I realise aloud.

"Yes," Wehi agrees. "We call them paths. Quickly now, we should not leave Karkinos waiting."

I squelch after Tasi, wishing I'd spared a moment to change out of my pyjama bottoms. To take my mind of it, I try counting the pools as we go but they stretch off between the trees, far beyond my sight. Do they all lead to other karkinoi colonies? That thought makes me marvel all the more. Another twinge in my chest, snatching my breath. I wish Mary could see this.

Tasi scuttles around a hedge of palms, I follow. And stop. My stomach drops to my knees.

We've stepped into a large clearing as long as a football pitch. Palms and ferns line the expanse, walling the sandy throne room in. There are no other crabs in sight, except one.

And it's the largest crab I've ever seen. Ever heard of. Could even imagine.

Coral red, its body would dwarf my house, front yard *and* back yard combined. Its back legs are tucked under it, its mid-legs— thick as palm trees—are relaxed on the earth. But its two pincers are spread wide, claws open, in greeting or affront I can't tell.

Tasi waves a claw at me, indicating I should follow. My legs turn weak. Now, of all times for an episode. I shuffle forward, cool sweat mixing with the warm seawater on my skin. We stop short of the Queen, and what I took to be beady eye stalks from across the room, reveals itself as a crown of eyes and thorny shell.

"Remember to bow," Wehi whispers in my ear.

I pull my stare away and drop to one knee. *What do I say? Should I say anything?* I clear my throat, open my mouth—

"Welcome, Landwalker Roy."

The voice surprises me. I'd expected it to boom; to rattle my bones and reverberate in my chest. But instead, it's smooth, soft; pitched exactly as it needs to be and not a decibel higher.

"It-it's an honour, Queen Karkinos." I garble out, heart in my mouth.

"Rise, come, I want to see you better."

With more effort that I'd like to admit to, I struggle back up. Then I suck in a breath, look up into her face and step closer.

122

Her features are similar to Tasi's. A strange, but humanoid face in an arthropod head. With her this big, I'm able to make out details that I hadn't seen before. A hooded brow, eyes slightly further apart than I'm used to. Instead of skin, her face is all armoured plates, which don't allow for much expression. On her chin, her antennae-beard is long and each one flicks about, reminding me of a snake's tongue scenting the air. One of them reaches out, touches my head.

I freeze again, holding my breath.

"You bested my Guardian," the Queen says.

I try not to cringe. "It was an accident," I say, then add a hasty, "your majesty." And dip my head.

"Nonetheless, beat him you did. And the messengers tell me you have refused to trade." Her attention shifts to Tasi, who shrinks into the sand. "*Why?*"

Wehi tugs my earlobe. "Set me down, Roy of Land, if you'd be so kind."

I lift her off my shoulder, cupping her in both hands and place her on the sand beside Tasi. My fingers shaking something chronic as I do—whether it's from nerves or disease I'm unsure. Mix of both probably.

"Queen Karkinos, if I may," Wehi says. "Roy of Land here has little need of the items we offered. He is ill, not long for the landwalker's world. But he does wish to trade."

"Oh?" That's got her attention. Karkinos shifts, a brief rise of her back legs as she moves her bulk forward a foot and leans in.

And as she does, a face—a *different* face—comes into view on the crown of her carapace. It's male, judging from the bristle on its cheeks. His eyes are closed, brows relaxed, sleeping-like. Or dead. My jaw slackens, but I manage to keep my mouth shut.

"What is it you seek that my karkinoi cannot give, Landwalker Roy?"

I'm too dumbstruck to answer. *There's a human face on the crab Queen's head.*

"Knowledge," Wehi speaks for me. "Roy would like to learn about the karkinoi. In exchange, he will trade us the Antikythera."

Antikythera? She must mean the heart. But I'm too distracted to do much else than stare at the Queen's shell.

Karkinos settles again, and as she does, I spot a new face, this one behind her foreleg, practically curling around the lip of her carapace. How many of them are there? Why? My stomach shrivels. What have I gotten myself into?

"Very well, Landwalker Roy. You may ask me three questions. Will that suffice?"

I drag my eyes away. "Y-yes." I place the safe on the sand. "I accept your trade."

"Very well," Karkinos gestures a giant pincer, and I try not to think about how easily her claw could wrap around my head and crack it like a walnut. "Please, ask your questions."

"I, uh . . ." I hadn't thought this far ahead. I search for inspiration and my gaze lands on the safe at my feet. "The heart, your Antikythera, what is it?"

Karkinos rocks back on her legs, her claws snap together with a 'whump' that I feel in my belly. "It is the heart of our people," she says. "The Antikythera measures the stars and moon, so we may work our magic."

I frown. "It's what allows you to use magic?"

"Is that your second question?" The Queen asks, tilting her body and head to one side. I glimpse another three faces on the back of her shell before I pull my eyes back inside my head.

"No, no!" I say quickly. Should I ask about the faces? Would that be rude? I still have two questions. I decide on another. "Tasi said a sea witch entrusted the Antikythera to you. Why?"

"It was she who made us. Long ago, she took us from the waters and taught us magic to help her." Karkinos' voice turns wistful, and her black eyes unfocus. "She was a marvellous teacher." She starts and shifts again, more faces flashing into view on her shell. "But even witches cannot live forever. Her life dwindled. She knew we needed a source to draw from to continue her work, so she forged the Antikythera, infused it with all her magic and gifted it to our keeping."

"I see . . ." No wonder it was so important to them. So why hide it in a wreck? Did they think it safe there? I'm tempted to ask, but I can guess the answer. No one really comes to our beach. Town was an hours' drive away, and Broome, the closest city, another four after that. Our beach has no facilities; no picnic or camping. Just a dirt road to the little house in the dunes Mary and I shared. But part of Karkinos' answer sticks in my mind. *The sea*

125

witch's work. What might that be? Did they call up storms on unsuspecting sailors? Turn the tides? My eyes light on the face at the top of Karkinos' carapace and my last question tumbles out of me before I can think.

"Why are there faces on your back?"

Karkinos turns her shell to me and I suck in a breath. My arms fall slack at my sides. I'd expected another face or two protruding from her back like the odd pimple. But this is . . . they are . . . immeasurable. Her shell is covered in them. Every last millimetre. Men, women, children, young, old, small, big. Hundreds, possibly thousands of faces. All of them sleeping.

"These are souls who were lost at sea," Karkinos says. "They are waiting to be reborn as karkinoi."

Somewhere in my throat, my voice croaks. Because my gaze has caught on a face in that mass of noses and cheeks, brows and chins. My vision narrows to a pinprick. Tasi, Wehi, the lockbox, even Karkinos, fade away; my focus is only on that face.

Impossible. My brain says.

Please let it be. My heart replies.

I swallow, the shake renewing in my hands. I flutter closer, drawn inexorably in. Fall to my knees. Is it?

It is.

"Mary?"

Karkinos moves before my hand can brush my wife's cheek. "Do not touch them."

126

And like that, Mary's turned away, out of sight. I stagger to my feet.

"Please, let me see her! Let me talk to her!"

"I cannot," Kariknos says. There's a slight edge in her tone—still soft, but firm, a warning not to argue. I try anyway.

"But—"

Pain shoots up my foot. I yelp, glance down, and find Wehi has one pincer clamped around my little toe.

Once she sees I've stopped, she releases her hold. "I am sorry, Roy of Land, but it is not possible. All the souls on Karkinos' back must sleep until they are reborn. They suffered in their last moments. It would be cruel to wake them as they are."

I imagine what it might be like to drown at sea and wake up trapped on the back of a giant crab. No limbs. No body at all. Perhaps they have a point. I slump into the sand, a hot ache spreading through my chest, up my throat. They are right. But Mary, my Mary, is there. Right there. And God, I miss her so much. So much it hurts.

My head presses into the sand as I prostrate myself before the Queen of Crabs. "Please," I whisper.

The responding silence cuts deep and twists in my stomach. Tears distort my vision. *Please.* I can't leave Mary behind. There must be a way. I search frantically. Mind whirring. "A trade!" I blurt. "Anything you want. Anything to free my wife."

That's what karkinoi are about, isn't it? An exchange of equal value? Eye for an eye. Or maybe . . . a soul for a soul?

127

Karkinos heaves a sigh, sinking down onto her legs again. "I cannot trade her freedom, Landwalker Roy," she says. "Would you have her haunt the seas? She is to be reborn as a karkinoi, as all karkinoi are."

As all karkinoi are? I blink. All karkinoi are born from souls lost at sea? I look to Wehi and Tasi for confirmation. Both of them nod. A new pain rises inside me, this one cold and bitter. Mary will be reborn while I am soon to die. Forever apart. No matter which way. I wipe my eyes. "Do they remember who they were?" I ask, turning to Tasi and Wehi crouched in the sand. "Do you remember?" *Would Mary remember me?*

Wehi's shell rocks from side to side, as if she's debating her answer. "I was cast off a cliff," she says at last. Her voice is so quiet I have to lean close. "I couldn't swim."

She leaves the rest unsaid, but it's enough to chill me to the bone.

Tasi scratches one foreleg with a pincer. "I was a cabin boy on a Dutch ship. We ran aground."

"I am sorry," I say. I shouldn't have asked. But I'd had to know.

Tasi shrugs his mottled shell. "When I hatched it was very fresh. Very painful. But now," he pauses, claws opening and closing as he thinks. "Now it is like remembering a story I heard long ago. There is no more pain."

"I see." And I do. If Mary has the chance to live a new life, one that helps ease the shock of her death, who was I to take that

128

away? The ache in my chest builds, but I know I am right. My eyes sting and I swallow, try to speak again, but a sob labours out instead. *Get up*, I tell my body. *Take your leave.* This is for the best. For Mary. But all my failing muscles do is shake. I am drowning, but not in water. My fingers clench the sand into fists. Why is it so hard?

Something cool falls on my hand. A mottled claw. Tasi, his blue shell bright in the moonlight. "Would you be willing to make a different trade, Roy?" he asks.

"A different trade?"

Tasi beckons Wehi with a foreleg. She scuttles over and they bow their shells together as words too quiet from me to hear pass between them. Wehi nods, murmurs something; Tasi pauses, then shrugs his claws.

"Very well," Wehi says, and they break apart once more. She turns to Karkinos. "We wish to propose a new trade."

Karkinos rocks back on her hind legs and one massive claw strokes her antennae-beard. "Go on."

"Roy of Land has proven himself a formidable force," Wehi says. "What is more, he has shown himself honest and respectful of our ways."

Where are they going with this?

Tasi rises onto all his legs. "I, we, wish employ his services to protect the Antikythera."

I stare at them. "I'm just an old man—"

Wehi's claw shoots out, pinches my arm. Hard. Shut up.

Karkinos eyes her two subjects, then me, and the air turns heavier under her scrutiny. "What do you propose in return?" she asks.

"Turn him into a karkinoi. Let him be with his beloved when she hatches."

Wait? What? My heart thuds in my chest. Me? A karkinoi?

The Queen is silent, her claw still stroking her antennae. "This is no small asking," she says. Her body shifts, sending shivers through the sand as she turns on me. "And you are not a lost soul."

My insides turn to ice. Do they mean to drown me? I might be dying already, but I don't want to drown. But . . . if it meant I could be with Mary again. Could I go through with it? Hope and terror set my heart racing. This is moving too fast.

"It is not enough," Karkinos announces, "and it is not our way to take life," she adds with a glare at Tasi and Wehi.

Just like that, in a few words, the little flame of hope I'd been cultivating splutters and dies. With a mute nod, I pull myself onto my feet. My legs shake, but I manage it. Sensing my time is up, I bow. "Thank you for hearing me out, Queen Karkinos."

Karkinos rises, this time to her full height, dwarfing me in her shadow. "Walk with me, Landwalker Roy," she says suddenly and starts down the sandy throne room.

I blink, sure I heard wrong. Walk with her? A glance at Tasi and Wehi and they bob their claws in the affirmative, and gesture for me to follow. I hurry after the Queen. Her gait is slow, methodical; every step considered. Even so, I have to coax my muscles into a shuffling jog to keep up with her.

She leads me past the pools, her legs picking and placing between the ponds with care, until we find ourselves on a beach. Gentle waves lap the shore, and Karkinos lowers her bulk onto the sand with a sigh.

"I am willing to grant you this trade," she says, without preamble. "But I need you to do something for me."

From this angle, the moonlight catches her face and I'm struck by how tired she looks. I sink down beside her, unsure of the protocol here.

"If it means I can be with Mary, I'll gladly do it."

"Careful, Landwalker Roy, you don't know what I'm asking yet."

My chin lifts. "I meant what I said. Grant me this wish and I'll do anything you want."

The weight of her gaze returns as she inspects me. "Karkinoi are born from souls lost at sea," she begins. "But not all of them can become a Queen like me. In fact, very few can."

I tilt my head. Where's she going with this? "Why not?"

"Because they did not choose this life," Karkinos says. "We give it to them, and many are happy to take it, but they don't choose. Queens like me chose this; we agreed to our fate before we died."

The heft of her words sink in. *Before she died.* Like all karkinoi, she too, had once been human. I open my mouth, not sure I want to ask my next question.

"Are you saying . . ?"

"I want you to take my place, Roy." Her black eyes fix on me. "Become Karkinos."

"But I-I'm not even female."

The Queen laughs, an odd gurgling noise through her mouth. "Male, female, it does not matter. What matters is that you are willing. That when your time comes, you go peacefully."

My mind gallops to catch up. "You mean . . . you *won't* drown me?" I can't help but feel a glimmer of relief at that.

"A violent death would mean you could not soothe the souls on your back as Karkinos."

Cool sand presses on my palms as I lean back to think. I'm no leader. Hell, I've barely a handle on my own life. Managing things was more Mary's talent. She had a way with people. My gaze slides to Karkinos' shell, landing on the face I've missed every day for the last eight years. I'm no leader, but if I agree to this, Mary will be there to guide me.

Perhaps she's been guiding me all along. To here. Now. This choice.

"What will happen to you?" I ask Karkinos.

Her foreleg traces lines in the sand, and suddenly I see the shape for what it is, dredged up from a memory of Mary and I sitting on our verandah one night, and her pointing the constellation out to me. Cancer, the crab. "I will move on," she says. Her eyes turn skyward. "My love is up there now, and I wish to join her."

A pang rises in my chest. I know that pain.

Rising to my feet, I brush the drying sand off my pyjamas and rest my hand on her enormous claw.

"I'll do it."

Five years later.

I wake to a tap-tap on my nightstand. Open my eyes. Tasi. Strange. He's come early this month, he normally doesn't visit before the full moon.

"What is it?"

Tasi spreads his pincers—a karkinoi's smile. "It's time," he says.

I sit up. "Oh." Hope quickens inside me. "Really?" I sit up. My body feels good. Fresh. "Should I bring anything?"

A shake of his body. No. "Just yourself. She's waiting."

Excitement bubbles inside me and I swing out of bed. No pain. No aches. A good sign. I leave the lights off as I move through my home. Finding my way by moonlight has become habit these last few years. I steal across the lounge, wincing at the creak of floorboards. A soft snore comes from the guest room; Keegan and Melissa haven't roused. I'm sorry to leave them like this, but it can't be helped. I step out onto the verandah.

"Grandpa?"

I turn. My granddaughter Zoe stands on the threshold in her nightie, blinking away sleep. She's small for a nine-year-old, but every day she grows more and more like Mary. Headstrong. A girl who knows what she wants.

"Where are you going?" she asks.

I drop to one knee and grin. "Off to be with your Grandma. Be good to your parents, eh, kiddo?" I rustle her hair. "I love you. Don't you forget that. Now go back to bed, before you wake your Da, eh?"

A frown creases her forehead, but she nods, and shuffles back inside the house.

I pace across the dunes, over the last rise and stop, not quite believing my eyes.

Crabs *cover* the beach. Every inch of it. Thousands, perhaps tens of thousands. All shapes and sizes and species; shells glinting and gleaming in the moon. I step out past the high-tide line and they move, parting like a curtain to bring me to a familiar looking hermit crab waiting with Tasi at the water's edge.

"Wehi," I say and bob my arms in an imitation of a karkinoi greeting.

"Roy," she says, returning the gesture. "It is good to see you again."

We walk into the water, Tasi, Wehi and I. Wehi on my shoulder, Tasi perched in my palm. The water surges around my legs, pulling me deeper, and I feel the urge to look back. I hesitate. Then a claw pinches my ear.

"Mary has something she wants me to tell you," the hermit crab whispers.

I cock my head. I'm listening.

"Let it go."

Tears spring to my eyes. "Yes, I will."

I step into the waves. Close my eyes and the sea sweeps me up.

I'm coming Mary.

Back in the beach house, my body cools. Heart attack, the doctors will say. No mistaking that pain in my chest last night. My memory wanders along the hall, across the patio to the shore. There's a small parking lot here now, and a boat ramp; a couple of science research vessels are shacked up on trailers for the night. It took a lot of work and lobbying to get them here, and the discovery of a loggerhead sea turtle nest in the area, but Keegan and I managed it.

A path leads from the boats down to the beach. And as my spirit quickens and hardens into its new shell, I smile, thinking of the sign planted on the shore.

Mary Quin Marine Reserve. Fishing strictly prohibited.

About the Author:

Nikky grew up as a barefoot 90s child in Perth, Western Australia, before moving to New Zealand in 2016. By day she works as a professional content writer and by night authors speculative fiction, often burning the candle at both ends to explore fantastic worlds, mine asteroids and meet wizards. Her creative work has appeared in magazines, on radio and in anthologies around the world. She is currently writing a dark fantasy trilogy, routinely sacrificing literary darlings to the editing gods in the hopes of seeing it published.

You can find her online at:
W:nikkythewriter.com | T:@NikkyMLee | F:nikkythewriter

LOYALTY TO A FAULT

Neen Cohen

The water pushes into my lungs.

Pain burns my heart, pumping agony to my limbs.

Air. I need air.

But she needs it more.

The moon shimmers, misshapen and taunting as it glides above my watery grave. I scream as claws from beneath reach for me.

A new day. Disorientation.

My legs push against an unseen force.

My hands blister as I push the sun across the sky.

We fall.

I push her away from the consuming water and watch as she sets, in a blaze of orange and pink.

Sacrificing myself for her. My eyes close.

The water pushes into my lungs.

About the Author:

Neen Cohen is an LGBTQI and speculative fiction author. She's been published through several publishers including Black Hare Press, Little Quail Press, Camden Park Press, and NBH Publishing. She has a Bachelor of Creative Industries and is a member of the Springfield Writers Group.

Neen lives in Brisbane Australia with her partner, son and fur babies. She loves to roam cemeteries, botanic gardens, and construction sites and can often be found writing while sitting against a tree or tombstone.

Check out her latest adventures and upcoming publications over on her Blog: https://wordbubblessite.wordpress.com

THE KEEPER

Deeanna West

The crabs were restless. More so than Aaralyn had ever seen them before. She sniffed at the current like Grandmama had taught her, searching for anything that would explain their behaviour. But there was nothing out of the ordinary. Salt and seaweed swirled, and whale song filled the waters as they migrated past the city.

"What's wrong with you?" she asked the crabs, not really expecting an answer, but it wasn't like there was anyone else to talk with.

Pearl looked up at her. The tiny pink crab was perched atop a fan coral, almost at eye level. Her eye stalks swiveled, and legs shifted their grip over and over. Her tension was palpable.

Aaralyn stroked her shell. "Hush now it's fine. Look, no one else is fretting as much as you."

The other crabs, Moon, Emerald and Ruby, had retreated into the coral bommie that was their home. They stared out at her and

Pearl, but none moved. It made sense, Aaralyn supposed, as Pearl was the representation of the goddess of loyalty. If anyone was going to continually try and warn her of danger, it would be Pearl.

Beyond the usual coral formations and rolling fields of anemones, the soaring towers of the imperial palace rose. It was the crowning achievement for the merfolk and Aaralyn had long thought it looked more like a beautiful statue than a functional palace. Barnacles sewn in hues of gold spiralled around the turrets, catching the last rays of sunlight filtering down from the surface, and corals had been cultivated into sprawling gardens. As far as she could see, there were no enemies riding in with their army of sharks, or landwalker ships bent on polluting their homes.

"It's okay, Pearl," she whispered. "Nothing is going to hurt you. Now it's bedtime, so you go and snuggle in with the others and I'll see you in the morning."

The little crab obeyed, leaping off the coral and letting herself float down to the seafloor. She was the smallest of the four, so was able to easily squeeze in beside Ruby.

Aaralyn packed the conch shells she'd been listening to back into her bag, preparing to return home for the night. She hadn't thought she'd enjoy the stories they contained when Delphia, her best mer, had recommended them. But she was hooked from the first daring adventure of the treasure hunting merman, Yara. There were ten conches out already, and if she wanted to catch up to Delphia she had to spend all her spare time listening to them.

140

A smear of silt fell from the last conch as she scooped it off the ground. It settled on her tail, marring one of the pale pink patches. She dashed it away, letting her hands trail on the other colours as she did so. Red, green, white and pink. Brilliant swathes of colour in the same shades as the crabs. A permanent bodily reminder of her destiny. She couldn't help but smile. She had begged Grandmama since she was four to allow her to watch the crabs, and, after the accident, she had thought she would ignore the rule that said she had to come of age first. Everyone had been shocked when Grandmama kept working despite not being able to swim. Waiting until she came of age had been torture, but worth it. She'd been keeper for a week, and it was the best week of her life.

The house was deep in the shadows of the palace by the time Aaralyn arrived home. The luminescent algae lining the windows cast soft pools of light into the water, guiding her way.

"Grandmama, I'm home," she called.

"In here."

She followed the voice to the kitchen to find her Grandmama, Ginevra, scooping salmon eggs onto beds of seagrass. She took the plate offered to her and let herself sink onto a coral settee.

"How is Ruby?" Ginevra asked, picking at her seagrass.

Aaralyn smiled. The Crab of Tenacity had always been her Grandmama's favourite. They matched each other. She had never seen her Grandmama give up on anything. Ever.

141

"All of the crabs are fine," Aaralyn replied. Then paused before changing her answer. "Actually, they were a bit off today."

"Off?"

"They just seemed fidgety. Like something had them on edge."

Frowning, Ginevra stared at her granddaughter. "Well you need to find what's bothering them."

"Nothing is bothering them. There were no scents on the current, I checked just like you told me to."

"That's not how it works child," Ginevra sighed. "You know this. The crabs are linked to the gods. They see all planes of existence; they know things we don't. If they are upset, then something is there."

"There was nothing there."

"So, you think you know better than the gods?"

Aaralyn rolled her eyes. "No, of course not."

"Did you join with them?"

Aaralyn refused to look at her, staring down at her food instead. "No, I didn't. Whenever I try, it fails. I can't do it."

"You can. That is the magic of our family, of the keepers. You need to try harder."

"Grandmama, I'm trying as hard as I can. I can't do it. Maybe you should."

Ginevra sighed and looked up to meet her eyes. They were sad but there was understanding too. "Joining with the crabs is hard, I know that. But this is something I can no longer do. The magic is yours now and you will eventually learn to control it."

Aaralyn nodded and Ginevra smiled. "Well then, let's go and see what's bothering them."

"Now?"

"Of course."

There was no arguing with her Grandmama, Aaralyn had tried before. With a sigh she went to fetch Rip. It would take a good ten minutes to strap Grandmama into the harness so the hippocamp could carry her to the crabs. Then who knew how many hours she would be forced to stare into the crabs' eyes, trying to mix her magic with theirs until she could see what they saw. It wouldn't happen, but Grandmama would make her try and try and try. It was going to be a long night.

It ended up taking a lot longer than ten minutes to get Ginevra into the harness. Rip fought them the entire time. He wasn't used to being taken out at night. He snorted and thrashed his tail, eyes rolling. The breeder had warned them that he wasn't suitable, that there were hippocamp that would be safer for a paralysed mermaid to ride. But of course, Grandmama had loved his spirit and refused to be dissuaded. She had argued that he couldn't hurt her much further, she was already dragging around a useless tail. Aaralyn hadn't known what to say to that, so they ended up with a barely controllable hippocamp.

The crabs were already asleep when they arrived and Aaralyn bit down on a surge of envy. Her eyes itched and she thought longingly of her warm bed.

"Ruby, sweetheart," Ginevra called softly, but it was Pearl that swam over.

"Actually, this is better," Ginevra said. "You have more of a connection with Pearl. Feel your magic and let it flow to Pearl, and her magic will do the same. You'll be one and then you will know what is concerning them."

Aaralyn lowered her hand so that Pearl could nestle into her palm. Her brows furrowed and she tried to do as Grandmama instructed. She could feel the magic there, swirling deep within, all pink and sparkly, but whenever she tried to reach for it, it slithered away. Pearl stared at her, clearly waiting. Her temple throbbed as she strained, but it wasn't going to work. She gasped and looked away.

"The magic won't listen to me," she cried.

"Try again."

Darkness. Aaralyn could have sworn she was awake, that her eyes were open. She could feel the grit clinging to her eyelashes and the lingering burn from having such a late night. But everything was black. She sat up in the bed. Yes, definitely awake. Squinting, she fought to get her eyes to adjust, peering into the gloom where she knew the luminescent algae should still be glowing. Nothing. Fear lodged in her throat, refusing to shift no matter how much she swallowed. She had to get out, had to find Grandmama and work out what was going on. In a swift motion she threw back the blanket of kelp. Immediately, light filled the room and Aaralyn could only stare, gaping at her tail as the light shone from it. The glow pulsed in an even beat, consistent and unrelenting. It had never done that before.

"Aaralyn, are you ok?" Ginevra called.

Aaralyn swam into her Grandmama's room only to freeze in the doorway, eyes jumping from her tail to her Grandma's, watching as they both pulsed in time with each other.

"What's going on?" she whispered.

"It's the crabs. Something's happening. Something's gone wrong. We need to get to them. Now."

Her voice was brisk, forced out between clenched teeth as she tried to clamp down on her own fear. Aaralyn held out her arm, supporting Ginevra's weight to swim towards the stable.

"There's no time, we need to go," Ginevra insisted. Aaralyn watched in horror as she grabbed at Rip's mane and, clinging tightly, let the hippocamp drag her out of the stable into open water.

Aaralyn followed, gaping at the surface. Darkness writhed above the city. Like someone had scooped up silt and thrown it into a swirling current. It blocked out the morning sun, they could see its rays lighting the land in the distance beyond the shadows.

"What is it?" Aaralyn asked.

"I don't know," Ginevra replied. "Hurry."

145

Aaralyn's tail screamed in protest at their speed, but she didn't stop. She had to keep up with Rip in case Grandmama fell from his back. They didn't stop until they reached the crab's coral bommie. A merman was already there, staring at the dark flecks raining down on the corals. Pulling up beside the man, they gaped. The swirling darkness and the dark flecks falling from it were enough to command anyone's attention, but it was the crabs themselves that Ginevra and Aaralyn couldn't look away from.

All four of them were frozen in place, eyestalks straining in panic. As the dark flecks touched them, the colour leached from their shells leaving sickly grey spots in their wake. Marks of taint that seemed to grow as they watched.

"You're here." The merman turned to them and Aaralyn felt another burst of shock. It was getting to be too much to bear. The crown prince, Zulimar. Aaralyn had never seen him this close before. Grandmama sent reports to the Emperor to update him on the crab's health and occasionally had gone to the palace for meetings, but Aaralyn hadn't met any of the royal family. Zulimar's golden tail was well muscled, a testament to his warrior training. He was handsome, even with his dark hair unrestrained and floating on the current.

"Zulimar." Ginevra greeted him with a bow. "What are you doing here?"

"Father sent me to get you. The crabs influence is fading. Father is worried that we are losing the protection of the gods."

146

"We don't have time to discuss this with the Emperor," Aaralyn interrupted. "We have to help the crabs first."

"Aaralyn, there's more to this than you know," Ginevra whispered. "Usually you would find out the first time when you bond with the crabs."

Guilt flared hot in Aaralyn's stomach. She made it sound like she had failed, that she was missing out on some important part of keeper life because she hadn't bonded.

"What is it?"

"The crabs, they aren't just important because they are a direct link to the gods. Their magic, their influence, it keeps us safe."

"Grandmama, I know that already."

"No, you don't. The virtues we value, the ones the crabs represent, Tenacity, Loyalty, Sympathy and Imagination. They come directly from the crabs. Without them we lose those traits and crueller, negative personalities shine through. Without the crabs we will destroy each other."

Aaralyn couldn't help but gape. Her eyes found Zulimar but he just nodded sadly, confirming Ginevra's words.

"It's not freely shared information," he said. "Only you keepers and the royal family know."

"How could you not tell me this?" Aaralyn couldn't help the accusation. She felt betrayed.

Zulimar pointed into the pen. "I know this is a lot to take in. I struggled too when Father told me. But look at them. Whatever is causing this taint is killing the crabs. Pearl can barely move already. People will start manipulating each other soon."

Aaralyn frowned. This couldn't be happening. Pearl was beside herself with fear. Her beautiful pink shell had taken on a sickly sheen.

"Fine, let's go see the Emperor," Aaralyn conceded.

The Emperor wasn't on the throne when they entered the palace. Instead, Zulimar led them through a side door to where the Emperor leant over a desk. The surface of the desk was carved into a map of the seafloor with territories marked by tiny conch shells. From the look on his face it was a struggle to tear himself away from it. The emperor was an imposing figure in that small room and Aaralyn struggled to keep her attention on him. She wanted to bow and kneel and not meet his eyes. He had the same golden tail as his son, the royal tail.

"Ginevra, thank you for coming. I know it's difficult for you to get around now but it is good you're here. I take it this is our new keeper, freshly minted?"

Aaralyn dropped into a quick bow. "Yes, your highness. I'm Aaralyn."

He nodded. "We will see much of each other for your duties, Aaralyn. Now, this taint. Already my staff have become suspicious of each other. I received reports of a fist fight amongst the guards. The crabs' influence is fading and if we don't save them, we will end up destroying ourselves."

"Do you know where the taint is coming from?" asked Ginevra.

"It looks like its originating in the sea goblins territory."

Fear. It laced through Aaralyn's veins turning blood to ice and clenching her stomach. She wanted to run from the room, but she forced herself to stay, to pay attention.

"The goblins have long coveted our territory," the Emperor continued. "They have sent raiding parties to our villages, but they've been quiet of late. Too quiet. I think they've been plotting, and I think this is their plan come to fruition."

Silence greeted his words. They were horrible, the worst possible case but they made too much sense to be ignored. If the goblins destroyed the crabs, then they would have free reign to take over the mer kingdoms.

"We need to find the source of the taint and stop it, whether it is in goblin lands or not," Zulimar offered. "I'll go."

She didn't want to. Aaralyn really didn't want to, but she swam forward.

"I'm the Keeper. This is my responsibility. I'll go."

"That is acceptable," the Emperor agreed. "But Zulimar will accompany you. He is trained in battle and this is a threat to our very way of life. There can be no failing this."

Zulimar bowed to his father. "We will leave straight away."

Aaralyn turned and threw her arms around her Grandmama. "I'm scared," she whispered into her shoulder. "What if I can't save them?"

149

Ginevra patted her shoulder. "You won't fail. You will save them, I know it."

With a sniff Aaralyn nodded and let Zulimar lead her out of the palace.

"So, how's your first week of being the Keeper been?" Zulimar asked, breaking the silence they had been swimming in for the past hour.

Aaralyn hadn't meant to be silent for so long. She had wanted to drown her anxiety in idle chatter like she usually would. But her thoughts twisted and snared. This was her fault. The crabs had tried to warn her, and she hadn't taken it seriously. Who ignored a warning from the gods? A barnacle brain, that's who. And besides, he was the prince. What did you talk about with a prince? Probably fancy cutlery and foreign dignitaries or something else she had no idea about.

"So?" He offered again. "Anything crazy happened since you took over from your Grandmama? I mean apart from this calamity we're facing?"

"Ah. No, it's been good actually."

"That's great."

It was such trivial chatter, at odds with their mission, but somehow it helped lessen the fear that was gripping her heart. Zulimar smiled at her and she couldn't help the heat flare in her cheeks. She prayed he wouldn't notice her blush. Her keeper duties, and the training before that, hadn't left her much time to socialise with anyone, let alone boys. Even if she pretended he wasn't the prince, he was still a really cute mer.

"Thanks for coming with me," she whispered.

He nodded. "Don't thank me yet. Whoever organised this attack planned it well. If it was the goblins, they knew exactly what would destroy us. Like Father said, without the crabs the entire empire will be slaves to their negative traits. We'll destroy ourselves."

Aaralyn glanced at him. His words were strong, tactical, but his voice hitched slightly. He was just as afraid as she was. "We won't let that happen."

They continued to swim in companionable silence, broken occasionally as they got to know each other. The reef of the capital soon gave way to sandy seabeds interspersed with rocky outcroppings. The occasional shoal of fish swam past them, taking care to avoid the taint ever present overhead. An aura exuded from it, a malignant eminence that threatened to consume anyone foolish enough to touch it.

The trail of the taint led them to a fissure. Aaralyn squinted into its depths, eyes straining to see into the gloom cast by its soaring sides.

"We could try swim over it," she suggested.

Zulimar shook his head. "We can't. The taint is right above the fissure. We'd have to go through it and I, for one, do not want to find out what happens if we touch it."

"It looks creepy in there. Are you sure there isn't another way around?" She tried to keep the fear from colouring her voice, but it still wavered. Everything that was happening to her now was terrifying and she hated it. She didn't want Zulimar to see her afraid and think her weak.

"No, we have to go through." He smiled at her and offered his hand. "But I agree, it doesn't look very inviting. Though it is to be expected since it's the entrance to the goblin territory."

He said it so casually. Floating there, holding his hand out to her as if he hadn't just said they were heading into enemy territory. The sea goblins were savage. Aaralyn had even heard rumours that they would eat their prisoners.

"I guess that confirms the goblins did this then?"

He nodded. "The taint leads directly into their territory. I'd hoped it would swerve away but no such luck."

"It's suicide! They'll kill us!"

Zulimar reached out and took her hand. "We'll be quick."

Doubt made Aaralyn's forehead wrinkle. "Ok then. We go in, destroy the source of the taint and get out again."

"Exactly."

"Fine."

It was cooler in the fissure, the water temperature dropping from its isolation. The sun's rays struggled to reach this deep. Aaralyn and Zulimar kept hold of each other as they swam. For a moment Aaralyn thought she was the one maintaining the contact but periodically Zulimar squeezed her hand and she knew he was getting comfort from it too. The entire way she was convinced the goblins were about to ambush them. That they would leap down from the walls to devour their faces. Nothing happened. Her shoulders ached from the tension, but they passed through safely.

The land beyond the fissure was a maze of mountains and rocky caverns. Sparse sea grass struggled to grow in any available seabed and small shrimp scurried out of crevices to snatch at debris as it floated past. A clatter of stone broke the silence and they froze, tails moving just enough to keep them afloat. Aaralyn's heart pounded and Zulimar's hand tightened around hers.

"Did you hear that?" she whispered.

He held a finger to his mouth to shush her, eyes scanning the rocks around them. Slowly he released her hand to draw the trident that was strapped over his shoulder. Zulimar had just got it free when they appeared. Three goblins swarmed over the rocks, teeth gnashing and screaming war cries. Zulimar pushed Aaralyn behind the rocks. Blood filled her mouth with the taste of copper as a sharp pain flared. A rock, she'd hit a rock. For a moment her head spun and her tongue throbbed from where she'd bitten it, but she shook to clear the dizziness, desperate to see what was going on.

One of the goblins was already down, blood spilling from the jagged hole in its' throat only to be tugged away be the current. Zulimar grunted as another goblin slammed into him from the side. Aaralyn winced as they went down in a tangle of limbs, Zulimar trapped beneath the goblin's writhing body. He used the trident to fend off its snapping teeth while trying to free himself. A low growl dragged Aaralyn's attention to the side. The other goblin advanced on her. The gleam in its eye was scarier than the sharpness of its teeth. She couldn't help it, she screamed.

The goblin loomed over her, its body blocking out the light until it was a dark shapeless blob. A shapeless blob that was bent on murdering her. She screamed again and lashed out with her tail, but the goblin dodged it, so she squeezed her eyes shut. If she was going to die, she didn't want to watch it coming.

Warmth. It soaked into her for a moment and then a heavy weight took its place. She opened her eyes to find the goblin's body pinning her down, eyes ruptured by the points of Zulimar's trident. It didn't matter how hard she struggled, the goblin's body wouldn't shift. Blood and gore drifted from its ruined eyes. Her stomach heaved.

"Pull me out, pull me out!" she cried, unable to keep the hysterics from her voice.

Zulimar obeyed, dragging the body to one side. As soon as she was free, she vomited. She hadn't broken her fast this morning, it hadn't even crossed her mind with the taint and the crabs and everything. Her stomach was empty, yet it demanded to be purged. She heaved and retched but produced nothing. Zulimar patted her back and stroked her hair. Finally, she straightened, dashing her mouth on her arm as she did.

"Thank you," she whispered. It wasn't enough. He had saved her life while she cowered behind a rock. She had been useless.

She wanted to say more, to express her gratitude but the words wouldn't come. So, she fell into him, arms wrapping around him and hoping he understood. He hugged her back and they floated there for a moment, heartbeats and ragged breathing calming in their closeness.

When they broke apart, Zulimar took her hand once more. "Let's go."

As they swam away, Aaralyn couldn't help but notice the body of the goblin that had been attacking Zulimar. It looked like he had stabbed his trident straight through its chest.

It wasn't much further. The taint lowered until it disappeared into the opening of a cave, combining with the darkness within until they could no longer differentiate it.

"We don't have a choice, we have to go in," Aaralyn said.

Zulimar nodded. "This is the end of the path. Whatever is responsible for the corruption will be in there."

They swam forward, Aaralyn's still-glowing tail lighting their way. Algae grew on the walls of the cave, but it wasn't the luminescent type that was so prevalent back home. This species was a deep green interspersed with red flecks.

"Don't touch it," hissed Zulimar, pulling her onwards.

After what seemed like hundreds of meters the tunnel opened into a larger cavern. A purple glow lit the area emanating from a large amethyst crystal. Pale coral had grown up from the sandy floor to create a pedestal for the crystal. Dark tendrils swirled around the stone.

"This crystal is the cause?" Aaralyn muttered.

"How can a crystal cause so much damage to the crabs?" Zulimar asked her. "They are the embodiment of the gods, surely they wouldn't be susceptible to something like this?"

"The crabs are basically immortal. They will live forever unless something injures them, or they get sick. That's why my family exists. The keepers make sure the crabs survive."

"Because without them the empire succumbs to chaos."

"Apparently."

Curiosity made Aaralyn swim closer to the Amethyst. They needed to destroy this thing. But how?

"I'm going to smash it," announced Zulimar, drawing his trident.

Something gnawed at Aaralyn. A doubt that made her hesitate. "Zulimar I don't think—"

She didn't finish. With a grunt Zulimer stabbed at the crystal, leaning his weight behind it. As soon as the trident connected with the shimmering purple surface, the shadows intensified. The dark tendrils exploded out from the Amethyst slamming Zulimar backwards. He collided with the cavern wall with a sickening crunch that brought tears to Aaralyn's eyes. She raced to him, but he waved her off, letting his tail push him back up.

"I'm ok," he grunted.

Cautiously, Aaralyn turned back to the crystal. Fingers quivering, she stretched out a hand to brush the blackness. Ice stabbed into her and she gasped, jerking her hand back. The skin on her hand was pale. A sickly hue marring her flesh the same way it had discoloured the crab's shells. Her magic stirred as she stared at it. Pink reaching for black, drawing it into her. She knew then. Knew what was required and her heart sank. Tears threatened but she sniffed them back. She had been useless when the goblins attacked but now it was her time.

"Zulimar," she said, still facing away from him. "Zulimar you need to leave now."

"What? I'm not leaving, we need to destroy this thing."

"No, we don't, we can't."

"Aaralyn I don't understand." He swam up to her, grabbing her hand and pulling her to face him.

"It can't be destroyed. The Darkness. Even if we break the crystal the darkness is out, it will continue to flow into the crabs until the taint overwhelms them completely. Our people, all the mermaids will be lost."

"How do you know that?"

"I know."

"But how?"

"My magic lets me join with the crabs. I've never managed to do it. But just now, I felt it. I felt their fear and they told me what to do. I know. You need to leave."

He frowned at her, still not letting go of her hand. "What are you going to do?"

"The darkness needs to go somewhere. If not into the crabs, then somewhere else. It needs to go into me."

His horrified look mirrored what she was feeling inside. She wanted to scream and rage and swim away. For a moment she pictured the life she could have led. Growing old like Grandmama. Maybe she and Zulimar could have been friends. Or more. But she was a keeper, and this was her duty.

"Go."

Indecision warred on his face. He wanted to stay with her, and she couldn't bear it.

"Go!" she screamed, already reaching for the crystal.

He obeyed, strong tail propelling him out of the cavern quicker than Aaralyn had expected. He'd been swimming slower for her this whole time. Tears flowed then, streaming down her face to mix with the water.

Her hand joined with the crystal, palm flat against it the ice returned. Her body went numb as the darkness flowed into her. She could sense its current. Feel as it pulled out of the crabs to stream into her instead. She smiled. They were safe. More and more corruption filled her, and she stared as her tail changed. The glow snuffed out leaving only the sickly purple light of the Amethyst as the patches of colour she had been so proud of faded, turning her scales a sickly grey green. The pallor of death clear as her skin turned cold. Her heart slowed as the last of the tendrils entered her fingers. Empty now the amethyst shattered, plunging the cavern into the dark.

Aaralyn floated there, completely still. She could feel the night coiling around her. Could sense the goblins moving outside. In the distance the crab's aura shone like beacons, but she couldn't remember why that was important. Nothing was important, here in the dark.

About the Author:

Deeanna West is a fantasy author writing from sunny north Queensland. If a book has magic, strange and amazing creatures or a world completely different to our own, then she's sold. When not holed up writing, she can be found playing games on the Xbox or out riding her horse.

JUST BETWEEN YOU AND ME

C.E. Rhoden

There's a ghost trapped in a castle in, um, Scotland I think it is. He was walled up into a cellar by his family. They stuck him behind bricks and mortar to starve to death because he was a coward. It's a famous story. Maybe you've heard of it? Well, that's not me.

I'm not walled into a cellar because, for one thing, this house doesn't have a cellar, and for another thing, it's made of weatherboard not bricks, and for a third thing, I'm not trapped.

Yes, fair point, I am stuck inside the walls, but that's my choice. That makes a lot of difference, wouldn't you say?

And for a final point of difference, my family didn't kill me. Well, I suppose they did in a way. All right, you could say that my father killed me, but also that he didn't. My own death is a thing I did myself. It was my decision, the actual end. He just made sure that I had no other choice.

You might think that because my father practically murdered me—except for the actual killing, of course, which I did myself—that I wouldn't want to hang around this house. But you'd be wrong.

Oh, did you hear that? "Hang around this house!" That's hilarious, because that's what I did. It is funny, really. No? Well maybe you had to be there. Wait, I'm getting back to why I'm here. You can learn all about my death later.

You really should know a few things if you are going to take over this place from my dad. It's not fair otherwise. I have to tell you my story.

I'm here inside the walls because it's where I like to be. I go sideways, see, and even though they can't see me, I'm pretty sure that my parents know I'm here. I hope they do. My father certainly hears me in the night—I make sure of that—and sometimes my mother looks right at me, exactly at the part of the wall where I'm hiding.

Of course they can't see me. I'm all spirit now.

If they could see me, I'd look like one of those Egyptian paintings. Have you ever noticed how they all walk edgewise? Their heads are in profile but their bodies face the front. That's because they move like me—looking over one shoulder to see where they'll go next, and stepping along a narrow path with their backs to the wall. Sideways like a crab. They extend their hands out to either side, just like I do, feeling the way.

I think those blokes were probably stuck inside the cavities between the walls of those pyramids. Yes I know they've never been found. I think that's because they didn't get mummified like the fancy pharaohs, as they were just extras. You know, making up the numbers. Not important. And no mummification means no bones, right? No nothing. All turned to dust centuries ago.

It doesn't actually take centuries to turn to dust, you know. Well, you might not know, but I do. Believe me. A couple of decades is enough if conditions are right.

Oh, the hanging? It was neat, you see. I climbed out of my window and onto the roof. The window was locked but I broke the pane. My dad was going to put some bars over the window, but he hadn't got around to it. He was planning to do it once he got back from Melbourne, to keep me imprisoned until the sailing date. So much for his plans.

It was easy. Out of the window, onto the roof, wrap my long-enough-but-not-too-long rope around the chimney—my rope made of school tie and shoelaces and winter scarf and belt, and even the strips of wrapping I had for boxing at school, those long calico bandage things that I used to bind around my knuckles under my boxing gloves. Did I tell you that I hated boxing? Not that it matters now. My dad wanted me to do it.

I used the boxing wraps around my throat, good and tight, like I was bandaging a wound. Then I slid off the roof and dangled from the eaves for a while.

163

It took longer than I thought it would.

You'd like to know how I ended up inside the wall cavity, I suppose, instead of tidily in my grave. Don't worry, my parents didn't chop me up and slip me in between the plaster and the frame or anything. I already told you, I chose this myself. I never wanted to leave home, see. They would have got rid of me any way they could.

Luckily for me, our church doesn't let suicides rest in its oh-so-holy consecrated ground, so no kirkyard for me. No, my parents had to bury me deep down in the home paddock. They passed it off as family tradition, even though nobody's been laid in the cemetery on our property since the 1860s.

That's how I managed to get back into the house, the home my father threatened to throw me out of, when he found me kissing Jim our stockman. It was like he'd never seen men kissing each other before, which makes no sense because for one thing, my father had once been a soldier, and besides, we had gangs of shearers through every spring and some of those blokes always shared a bunk, you know?

I love my home and I never want to leave. I was all set to take over when my parents got too old. Me and Jim would have managed just fine.

But my dad didn't see it that way. When he came across us kissing in the stable he yelled for Morgan, our overseer, and together they bundled me into one of the loose boxes, the solid one where we stall the stallion when he's worked up. Then they did Jimmy over extra heavy. My mother came out to see what all the noise was but she got shooed back inside quick. Jim was screaming and I was shouting and Dad and Morgan kept beating, cursing and kicking and thumping.

That took longer than you would think, too.

Afterwards I heard them tell the other hands that Jim had got into trouble for stealing and quit in a huff, but I know he's never left the place. He's here too, but beat up so bad his spirit went back to its ancestors somewhere up country where he'll be safe. His bones are here, though, under the pigeon house, unless they've gone to dust, too.

I bet my parents are sorry now that there is only you to inherit the property, cousin. They thought they would have another son, a better one, but it's not easy to get a new baby in a house where there's an unhappy spirit. Especially when the unhappy spirit is the teenager that would've been its big brother if he lived that long. Little baby spirits are smart enough to keep away.

When my dad got back from Melbourne with our sailing tickets, I was already lying dead in the stable, which is a good place to be. You will see, it is a fine building with a bricked over floor and a big wide loft. My dad's plan was to sail us to India where my mother's brother was doing some fancy government job. They planned to leave me in India to live in disgrace and never return home.

Only when I was dead, and with no little brothers, well then my mother's younger nephew in India would be the one to inherit the station. But you know that because that's where you come from, that's you.

My dad will never be rid of me and I guess you won't be rid of me either because this house will never be rid of me. I'm no trouble, even if I am interrupting your dream tonight. I promise I won't make kissing noises in the wall, or whisper Jimmy's name along the lining boards. I won't sob or moan or rattle the rafters. You just leave me be, and let Jimmy lie, and we will stay quietly here at home for always.

You maybe won't remember talking to me, cousin, but here is something you really should remember, just between you and me.

Make sure you ask my mother to tell you about the local girls, maybe get some introductions when you go to church tomorrow, or go to the hall when they have a dance. Get yourself a girlfriend of any sort, I'm telling you.

About the Author:

Clare Rhoden lives in Melbourne Australia with her husband and a highly intelligent poodle-cross called Aeryn.

Clare is an author, blogger and book reviewer inspired by politics, culture and history. Her novels include historical fiction 'The Stars in the Night' *and the dystopian trilogy* 'The Chronicles of the Pale.' *You can find Clare's books, blog posts and reviews at* https://clarerhoden.com.

THE SELKIE

Lisa Rodrigues

As the net falls over me, my scream is torn away by the squall. Nobody can hear me in this place, a small beach between a cliff face and the churning sea. I thought the hour was too late for humans to roam, and I curse my foolishness. As my captor clambers from his hiding place, I try not to glance at my second skin, a shapeless lump on the sand.

"What do you want with me?" I ask, trembling with rage. The net is rope and seaweed, but it burns like frozen iron.

"Great lady, I mean you no harm," he says. His steps sink into the sand a few feet away, hands out as if approaching a wild animal. He is right to be afraid.

He seems both exhilarated and shocked at his catch. His gaze falls lower to my nudity and my stomach turns. I resist the urge to cover myself with my hands. Then he averts his gaze, abashed.

My relief lasts only a second before he glances towards my second skin. It must look like a discarded cloak to him, but if he touches it I'm doomed.

In desperation, I scream my question again and am left panting. He looks like a simple man, but the air within my prison tastes like burnt hair and rotting weeds. Magic.

He falls to his knees, presses his windswept forehead onto the sand and stammers his request. He is a poor fisherman's son with dreams of becoming a storyteller. Alas, he has no story of his own. He learned of ways to trap a selkie as she changes, and he longs for my secrets.

"My lady, please tell me your story, and I will set you free." His cheeks are flushed and his eyes are fervent in the fading light. He is as young as I was when I chose the sea.

Men often lust for my kind, and there are traditional wiles to free myself from them. Magic is not usually involved, but the air in my prison is thick with it, sapping my strength as he speaks. When he is done I can only say "please" and fall to my knees.

I see a decision in the twitch of his jaw, but I'm too weak to move as he closes the gap between us. When he removes the net I want to fight, but my muscles only shudder as I take grateful gulps of fresh air.

He starts towards my selkie skin. Magic means knowledge, so he knows that taking my skin traps me on land. What he may not know is that any human contact with a selkie skin can destroy it.

THE SELKIE

I try to stand, but my legs won't hold me and I fall, sprawled but reaching towards him. He picks up my skin. My eyes close and my body sinks into the sand, defeated.

Warmth fills me, and I wonder if it's the embrace of death. My eyes flutter open. I'm surprised to see my skin lying over me intact, and the man looking at me. He smiles when he sees me revive. He's careful not to remove my selkie skin when he lifts me and walks me towards the surf.

As the sea reaches up to cradle me, my blanket skin warms me from above and I savour the heat of him as he cradles me to his chest. I feel held as I haven't since I was a human babe, and the memory shocks me. I could twist out of his arms and slip away, but I stay.

He kisses me on the forehead and loosens his grip. His eyes glint with a glimmer of gold, reflecting the stars above.

Before he releases me, I place my hands around his face. His eyes shine with joy at my recovery, and then cloud with uncertainty. I'm not hurting him, but my strength is returning, and my gaze is direct and clear. I could break him now.

I command him instead. "I will meet you while the crab is in the sky." Then I twist in his arms, wrap my skin around me and disappear into the waves.

My body is still weak and I am missing my kin, but I will return to him soon. I will tell him my story, how I too once longed for more than my human life. He touched my second skin, and the stars are in his eyes, so I know he was born under Poseidon's favoured sign. For a few more nights the path is raw, and he will have a choice, as once was offered to me. He can leave behind his mortal life and become a selkie of the sea.

About the Author:

Lisa Rodrigues is a Eurasian Australian writer in her 30-somethings living in Perth. She's written speculative fiction on and off for years. She works fulltime in tourism marketing, and when she's not working or writing she can be found upside down doing acrobatics.

She's previously been published in literary journals and anthologies. You can find more of her work at endofnext.wordpress.com.

KLARIA'S BATTLE

Heather Ewings

Klaria watched as Pedro heaved the canvas sack onto his back.

"Will ye come to town this time?" he asked, as he always did.

Klaria shook her head, as she always did. "My bleeding time has come." She hadn't bled for years, but Pedro never seemed to notice she no longer hung her rags out to dry.

"No wee ones then?" Pedro's face fell.

"Sorry, love."

Pedro heaved the door of the bothy open, and headed out into the cool spring day.

Klaria followed him to the doorway, watching until he disappeared out of sight down the slight incline of the meadow.

Klaria avoided town. It was too close to the ocean. She couldn't control herself near the sea, the urge to take to the waves too strong. She'd already scared herself once by nearly drowning.

It turned out she wanted life more than she wanted to go home.

She went back to the house. Pedro had packed the butter and eggs for the market, but he'd left her a fish caught fresh from the river this morning, still splashing in the bucket in the shade of the verandah. Klaria retrieved her basket and headed out to the garden. Fresh fish with salad greens would make a good dinner, and there'd be enough to leave in the meat safe for a cold breakfast the next morning.

The day passed slowly without company.

Klaria weeded the garden and gathered the eggs, the murmur of the chickens a comfort in the quiet. She swept out the single room of their small house, and spread the blankets across the line to beat out the dust. As the day drew to a close she returned to the house, to gut and cook the fish before dark.

For the most part, Klaria was pleased she and Pedro had not had children. She'd determined it, after all, drinking the tea recommended by the wise woman to stop babies coming, certain one day she'd find her shell and be gone, and not wanting to abandon an infant with a bereft father.

But days like this she wished she'd not been so certain of that future. It would've been nice to have a handful of children to fill the silence of the days when Pedro went to town.

She'd never found her shell. She'd scoured every inch of the property, outside and in, probing hollow tree trunks and abandoned animal burrows, searching in the wall cavities of the house and shed, and under all the loose floorboards. Even under the ones securely nailed in place. Wherever Pedro had hidden it, it certainly wasn't here.

Dinner cooked, Klaria took her plate down to the river's edge.

The moon would be full, and she wanted to sit where its light would fall upon her as it first rose.

She could escape the sea, its pull not so strong here in the mountains. But she could not escape the moon, and the pull it exerted on her was far stronger.

Though she kept her gaze on her meal, her skin tingled when the moon first peered above the horizon. She held off from looking as long as she could, resisting the pull until she couldn't and she gazed up at the full round moon, her vision blurring with tears.

Once she'd gathered with the other crab-folk, and they'd shed their shells and danced upon the sand, frolicking under the moons rays.

Did they still do that, after all this time? Or had the human presence grown so large it was too dangerous?

She closed her eyes, letting two great drops roll down her cheeks.

If only she could see her family again.

As if in answer there was a scuffling at the water's edge, and she opened her eyes as a large rock emerged from the river and scuttled up the bank.

Klaria stared. She knew what it must be, and yet it was too unlikely to be possible.

She'd never known a crab to come upstream. They didn't like the fresh water, weren't strong enough to swim against the downward current.

Still, two beady eyes emerged from one end of the rock, and it paused, the eyes scanning the surrounds, coming to rest on Klaria. It sidestepped towards her on the stony bank.

She held her breath as it approached. Sure enough, before it reached her, it propped itself up on its four back legs, claws and two front legs waving in the air.

There was a distinct crack as the soft centre line of the undershell pulled apart, followed by much wriggling and squirming as a young, wet woman emerged from within.

At first she was small, child-sized to a human, but as she unfolded she stretched limbs and torso until she was almost as tall as Klaria.

She pulled herself to a sitting position, blinking a couple of times before her gaze landed on Klaria, and a beaming smile broke across her face.

"Aunt Klaria. I found you!"

Klaria's heart pounded, and she blinked several times herself, an attempt to clear her vision from this unexpected sight. Twenty-five years had passed since she'd seen another of her people. Twenty-five years of settling into the certainty she'd never see them again.

"We need your help," the woman said.

"Who are you?"

"I'm Anabelle, Ninian's daughter."

"Ninian?" A lump formed in Klaria's throat at the sound of her younger sister's name. "Is she . . ?"

Anabelle shook her head. "She's fine. Scared, like we all are, but fine."

"Scared?" Klaria's heart increased its pounding. "Why are you scared?"

"The townsfolk are hunting us. We need you to come, to help us."

Klaria shook her head and pushed herself to her feet.

"I can't help you." She took a step backwards. "There's nothing I can do."

"You know the human's ways," Anabelle insisted. "You've lived with them for two dozen years. You can teach us what you know."

"I don't know anything. I've been living in the mountains, I only see my husband, and the few friends who drop in."

"He must talk," Anabelle said. "You would hear things."

"I don't have my shell." Klaria looked away, back at the house. Could she lock herself in?

She couldn't stand against the humans. She was weak, soft. Old. How could her people expect her to do anything?

Anabelle shook her head. "You don't need your shell to teach us what you know."

175

Klaria imagined the pitying looks of her kin if she returned in her soft human form, and her chest constricted. "I can't come back without my shell!"

"Please, Aunt. You must come."

"I can't."

"They're killing us, Klaria. No one believes in the crab-folk anymore. They forget we are human inside, as they are, and they hunt us." She reached out to grab Klaria's hand, forcing Klaria to meet her gaze. "They *eat* us."

Klaria swallowed against the lurching in her stomach. "What about the other crab-women in town?"

Anabelle's eyes grew wide, and she shook her head. "They're all dead. They pined away for the sea to the point where they died of heart break. You're the last still alive."

Klaria dropped back onto the bank, the breath knocked out of her.

"Seysill, Aine, Ena? Dead?"

Anabelle nodded. She squeezed Klaria's hand, and Klaria realised her niece was shivering.

She forced herself to stand. "You're so cold! Come inside. Let me find you a blanket."

Klaria lifted Anabelle's shell. It was large and cumbersome, awkward to wrap her arms around, and by the time they reached Pedro's hut her muscles ached.

Inside the fire was still burning low, and Klaria added a few extra branches, pulling the blanket from her bed to wrap around Anabelle.

"I never knew it would be so cold in the mountains." Anabelle pulled the blanket tight around her shoulders. "I can barely feel my limbs."

Klaria reached out and rubbed some colour back into Anabelle's arms. "I'll get you some tea, and you can tell me what's happening."

Anabelle's story lasted well into the night.

The human population had tripled in the twenty-five years since Klaria was first taken, their settlement spreading out along the shore, their buildings popping up in all the sheltered coves where the crab-folk had once gathered for their ceremonies. The humans hadn't liked to see the crab-folk dancing naked under the moon, and had chased them away, so now Klaria's people no longer gathered on the sandy shore, but on the rocky islands dotted off the coast, which were too sharp for the crab folk's soft human feet.

Where Klaria's childhood had been one of a truce between human and crab, Anabelle's early years involved a continuing cycle of loss. Family and friends were killed, at first while they danced upon the shore, and in later years in crab form, taken from the sea.

Klaria's stomach churned at the images Anabelle painted in her mind, her bile burning as it rose up in her throat, even as her cheeks were cooled with tears.

"You have to help us," Anabelle urged again. "You have to teach us what you know."

"I don't belong without my shell." Klaria shook her head.

"We found your shell," Anabelle said.

Klaria couldn't believe it. "How?"

"Your husband has it hidden in the inn where he sleeps when he visits town. My mother took human form, she—" Anabelle's eyes flicked away, but then her jaw set and she met Klaria's gaze again. "You should know. My mother seduced your husband. He told her how he loved you, as he made love to her, and when he left to go to the bathroom she searched the room. She said she felt it, as though you yourself were in the room with her. But your husband returned before she could retrieve it."

Conflicting emotions swirled, so many Klaria didn't know which one to grab onto. Her sister seduced her husband, and he gave in to it, though he swore he'd never lay with another woman. Why did she hurt so much about the infidelity of a man she tolerated, a man who'd kidnapped her in the first place? She shook those feelings aside. All the more reason to escape.

If she had her shell she would be free. She could escape the man, and the mountain, and return home.

"Can't she try again?" she asked Anabelle.

Anabelle shook her head. "It's too dangerous. We're not taking human form again, not until we know how to fight them."

A strange sense of calm swept through Klaria's body. Her shell had been found. With her shell, she could do anything. She could help Ninian, and Anabelle, and the rest of her people. She could lead them against the humans.

She looked at Anabelle. "Next full moon, Pedro will return to market. I will come with him. Gather everyone. I will find my shell, and I will return."

"You'll help us?" Anabella's whole face lit up.

Klaria nodded. "I'll help."

The month passed painfully.

Klaria wanted nothing more than to confront her husband with what she'd learnt, but what good would it do? He knew she never had visitors. He'd deny it, accuse her of paranoia. He might even refuse to allow her to join him the following moon.

Her days were spent arguing with herself, angry at her husband for laying with another woman, angry that the other woman was her sister, angry that Pedro had taken her shell from her in the first place.

But she was hurt too, and that baffled her the most. He was a foolish human who couldn't get a wife by any other means, and yet she'd grown fond of him, of all the thoughtful little things he did to make her life as comfortable as possible.

Everything except return my shell.

179

Finally the time came. Pedro heaved the sack up onto his back, and Klaria waited for him to invite her along.

He approached her, kissed her forehead, and turned to leave.

"I, uh—" Klaria began.

"Yes?" He turned. "Is everything all right?"

Klaria wrung her hands together. "I thought I might come with you, this time."

"You're not bleeding?"

Klaria shook her head. "Not today."

His eyes lit up. "Do you think there's a wee one on the way?"

Klaria licked her lips. Could she lie to him? She shook her head. "It's too early to tell."

He nodded, but still his eyes shone in a way they hadn't for years. "A son," he said. "To carry my name." He glanced at her. "And now your barreness has lifted, he will soon be followed by a daughter to carry yours."

He beamed, and Klaria forced a smile. Better to allow their last days together to be happy ones.

Pedro was not often talkative, but now his spirits were up he filled the walk to town dreaming about the future, about the rooms he would build onto the house, about how he would teach his child to fish, and garden, and hunt.

"They'll be self-sufficient like we are," he announced. "Not like the young folk in town, growing up with no idea how to care for themselves, nor what their place is in the world. That's what's causing all the problems in the world today. One day it'll all crash down around them, and then where will they be? Starving, that's where." He shook his head. "I'll have no children of mine in that position."

Klaria listened, nodding whenever he looked her way, making small noises of agreeance now and again, so he felt she was listening.

They reached town by nightfall, the moon fat and round on the horizon.

It called to her, as it always did, but now something else pulled her, too. Lapping at the edges of her senses were rivulets of energy, calling her home.

A strange longing overpowered her as they approached the inn, a pull that led her feet to the very place Pedro wanted to go.

The inn keeper gave her a strange look, but Pedro introduced her as his wife, and the innkeeper nodded.

It was all Klaria could do not to run to the room, and once in the room, not to seek out the hiding place where he'd hidden her shell.

Pedro set their bags down and knelt before the empty fireplace, scrunching up bits of bark into a ball and placing it in the grate.

"What can I do?" Klaria asked.

"Help me with the fire." He gestured to the basket of kindling. "It gets cold here at night. The chill wind whips off the water and sneaks in through the gaps, and these days my bones ache when it's too cold."

Klaria did as he asked.

Once the fire was burning brightly, she asked if she might go for a walk.

He grunted a reply, commenting that she could do whatever she wanted.

Outside the night air felt crisp against her face. Klaria pulled her shawl tighter around her shoulders and followed the narrow path to the shore.

With every step she fought the pull to turn back, to retrieve her shell. There was no point. She couldn't do it now, not with Pedro in the room.

She'd hoped to find the beach empty at this time of night, but there were people scattered all along the shore. Fishermen strode into the sea with long nets, muttering to each other. Further along a man paced, and when Klaria drew closer she saw he was holding a baby, patting its back in time with his steps.

He glanced at Klaria as she walked past, his eyes drawn.

She offered him a weak smile.

"Do you know how to get a baby to sleep?" he asked.

Klaria shook her head and kept walking.

There was a young couple further up, hand in hand as they strolled along the sea's edge, the waves lapping at their ankles. And further, around a curve in the coast, a group of young men loitering on the sand, the scent of ale carried on the breeze.

Was there nowhere where the crab-folk could come ashore in safety?

182

Klaria came to a stand of rocks, jutting out into the sea. The points were hard on her feet, but she followed them as far out as she could, until the sea splashed around her ankles and sent her feet slipping.

She flung out her arms, her heart racing as she steadied herself. It would do no good to fall into the water in her heavy skirts. Pedro would be angry, *if* she managed to pull herself out of the sea, and she couldn't help her people if she were dead.

She took a few steps back and sat down.

"Ninian," she called, her voice soft. "Ninian!"

It would take time for her call to be heard under the waves, time she wasn't sure she had.

Would Pedro be asleep? Or was he wondering where his wife was, and what she was up to?

Could he be suspicious of her sudden desire to join him in town, or did he truly believe she carried his child, that the connection would be enough to make her stay?

The moon was high in the sky now. The wash of the waves made Klaria want to dance, but if she did the human-folk would know by her movements she was truly crab and then there'd be trouble.

She wondered how her family coped below the waves, feeling the moon's presence, and yet unable to come to the shore.

The waves washed again, in and out. Was no one coming? She was about to stand when a crab scuttled up the rock.

Its eyes peered at her.

183

"Ninian?"

The eyes swayed ever so slightly, and Klaria felt a surge of panic that she had forgotten what her sister looked like.

"Is that you?"

One claw raised and snapped. Yes.

"Can you not change, for a moment?"

The eyes watched her for a moment, before the two claws raised and snapped together. No.

Klaria glanced around, realising the group of young men on the beach were on their feet, watching her. "I know where my shell is," Klaria said. "I'll find a way to get it. When I do, I'll be back."

Ninian's claws clacked together, two, three, four times, in quick succession.

Klaria nodded. "I'll be as quick as I can."

Back at the room, Pedro snored soundly. Klaria took a moment to peer under the bed, but the fire was nothing more than hot coals, and gave out little light. She pressed her fingertips against the floorboards, feeling for gaps or loose, wobbly boards.

Nothing.

Then she realised that the nails had been removed from the board directly beneath the bed's leg

Her breath caught.

It must be there.

She couldn't grab her shell now, but if she waited until Pedro went to market the next morning . . .

Klaria undressed and climbed into bed. Pedro snorted, and rolled over, a heavy arm crossing her shoulders. She forced her breathing into a slow even rhythm. Her shell was in her grasp.

Morning couldn't come fast enough.

Klaria tossed and turned, disturbing Pedro enough that he snapped at her in the early hours of the morning, taking most of the blanket with him as he rolled away from her, the bed rocking from his movement.

Klaria waited until his snores started up again, and then sidled up close, careful to lay extra still under the tiny portion of blanket available to her.

She didn't sleep.

When Pedro woke the next morning she slowed her breathing, listening as he climbed out of bed and pulled on his shirt and trousers.

There was silence for a moment, and then his lips pressed against her forehead, and she heard him add another log to the fire, before the door clicked as he left the room.

Klaria waited a moment longer. When there was no other movement she opened her eyes.

The room was empty.

She took a deep breath.

After all this time. If only she'd accompanied Pedro on his trips to market from the beginning! But she'd been so scared after that first time, when she'd nearly drowned trying to return to her home. When she couldn't find her shell at his home, she'd assumed he'd hidden it somewhere along the path to town, or else higher in the mountains. The task of searching such an area had seemed impossible, and she'd given up, too easily. She'd never imagined for a moment he'd leave it behind in the town itself.

She shook her head, and slid out of bed.

The bed was made of solid wood, bulky and heavy. Klaria pushed against it, satisfied to feel it shift under her effort. But then it bumped against something and wouldn't budge any further.

She knelt by the bed to try to manouvre the floorboard, but the bed hadn't moved far enough to move it, so she lifted the bed again, her muscles straining against the effort. Something seemed to be stopping the bed from moving.

She moved around to the other side of the bed.

There was a nail jutting from the floor, preventing the leg on this side from sliding any further.

Klaria bit her lip. She didn't have any tools to remove the nail, so instead she lifted the bed, heaving it towards her.

Sweat dripped into her eye, stinging. The fire flared, and she wished Pedro hadn't bothered to stoke it before he left.

Finally the bed slid easily, and Klaria slipped and fell, dropping the bed with a thud.

She froze, straining her ears but couldn't hear anything over the pounding of her heart.

When there was no movement in the hallway, she stood, taking a drink of water from the jug on the mantlepiece, forcing her breath to slow enough so she could hear over the beating of her heart.

All was still quiet out in the hallway, so she knelt by the odd floorboard. She could *feel* her shell through the thin strip of wood, reaching out to her just as much as she reached out to it.

There was no indent to fit her finger, but Klaria pushed on one end and the whole floorboard tipped upwards.

A waft of salty sea air reached her nose, and then Klaria saw it, the brilliant blue of her shell, visible under years of dust. She set the floorboard to one side and reached in, a current of energy zapping along her fingertips as she touched the hard surface, tears rolling down her face, creating shiny trails on the shell where they washed away the dust.

She had to press the underside of the shell up into the indentation of the back to get it up through the narrow gap, the legs and claws clattering against the wood as they came through.

"I never thought I'd find you again," Klaria whispered, her breath catching at just how her shell gleamed even after all this time.

"What have you done?"

The voice boomed. Klaria looked up to see Pedro crossing the room, his face red, the veins in his neck bulging. She hugged the shell as she stood, stepping away from Pedro's anger.

"I—"

He crossed the room in two strides, grabbing the legs of her shell and ripping it from her hands.

"No!" Her voice was a howl. "Please."

"I've kept you safe, all this time." He waved her shell in the air. "You're going to leave? Now you're with child? Is that why you stayed so long?"

It took Klaria a moment to understand what he was talking about.

She clenched her fists. "There is no child. There's been no bleeding for years, though you don't care enough to notice. I never stayed because I wanted to, I stayed because I had no choice." Her eyes darted from Pedro's face to her precious shell. "But now . . ." She lunged for her shell, and in the same movement he swung it back, flinging it into the fire.

Everything moved in slow motion.

Klaria's fingertips brushed a claw as she fell through the air, pain jolting up her body as her knees crashed against the floor.

The shell spun, round, and again, and once more, before it landed with a puff of ash and smoke among the flames.

Neither Pedro or Klaria moved for a moment, and then pain shot up Klaria's right side and across her back as flames licked the underside of the shell.

"No!" She pulled at her clothes a moment too long before she realised it was not her clothes that were burning.

"Save it. Save it!" She screamed at Pedro, who watched her wide eyed as she clawed at the pain now shooting across her face.

Finally he jerked into action, grabbing the poker to knock the blackened shell from the fire.

Klaria collapsed on the floor, her chest heaving.

"Love. I'm sorry. I didn't know." He was by her side in an instant, brushing hair from her face. "I didn't realise the stories were true."

He pulled on her shoulder. Klaria tried to push his hand away, but he was too strong and he rolled her over.

His hand covered his mouth as he recoiled. "Oh, Love. What have I done?"

Klaria brought her hands to her face. She flinched as her fingers brushed her cheek, the pain still raw though the burning sensation had stopped.

When she gingerly touched her cheek again there were bumps and valleys, her skin puckered from the heat.

Tears filled her eyes, and she scrambled for her shell.

Pedro just watched as she picked it up, examining the charred crack that almost split the shell in two, the crisp underside that had been soft and pliable moments before.

"What have you done?" she asked him, tearing off her blouse to swing the shell up and over her shoulders.

She waited for the sense of suction, pulling her back into her true form, but the hard edges of the shell just poked into her skin.

"What have you done!" She wailed, trying to somehow push herself inside the shell that wouldn't take her.

"What have you done?" She sank to the floor.

Her stomach churned, and she sucked in deep breaths of air that never seemed to reach her lungs.

"Love. I'm sorry. I didn't know." Pedro's gaze was pitiful.

Rage burned in the pit of her stomach and she pushed herself to her feet.

"You ruined me." She waved her shell at him. "You ruined my life. But I won't let you and yours ruin the lives of my people."

Pedro flinched, and Klaria stormed out, ignoring the stares of those she passed, peering out of their rooms. She strode to the beach, grabbing the first dinghy she could find. Throwing her damaged shell inside, she pushed it out into the waves.

Somewhere there must be a quiet space for the crab-folk to come ashore.

Klaria just had to find it.

There was nowhere.

Klaria rowed until her arms shook under the strain, but everywhere there were signs of human habitation. Small coves were watched by lonely cottages, while on the shores of larger bays houses snuggled together as though for safety.

How was she supposed to protect her people from humans, when the creatures were everywhere?

The oars slipped from her hands, and Klaria watched them float away before laying down in the boat, her gaze on the clouds above.

She was not human. But now, she was also not crab.

The sun beat down on her from above, the heat seering her skin. She welcomed the pain, which matched the intensity in her chest, the burning in her lungs as she sucked in each breath, and tearing in her heart as Pedro's act replayed again and again in her mind.

Who knew her shell could be damaged so badly, and she could still live?

She must have dozed, for she woke to the boat bumping against something solid.

The sun was even higher in the sky, her skin red from its rays. Her throat hurt, and her lips were dry.

She pushed herself up, blinking at her surroundings.

Across the waves she could see the coast, houses dotted all the way along. When she turned, she found herself at a rocky island, barely more than two dozen steps across. She climbed out on unsteady feet, leaving the boat to the current.

Movement in her periphery caused her to turn.

A crab scuttled along the shore towards her, then another lifted its beady eyes above the water, and it too emerged from the shallows. Soon she was surrounded.

"I failed," she told her family, showing them her damaged shell. "I can't help you."

A crab came close, grabbed the edge of her trousers with a claw, and pulled.

"I'm coming."

The crab released her, and scuttled towards the centre of the island, where the rocks were higher. Here Klaria found a rock pool, seawater and rain-water mixing and she lowered her mouth to drink great soothing gulps.

When she was done she sat in the semi-shade provided by the rocks, holding tight to her shell.

All around, more and more crabs gathered.

Klaria must have dozed again, for she woke to the sound of a hundred shells cracking.

All around her the crab-folk were emerging. They came to her, and held her in their arms, and they cried together for the loss of her shell, and for the loss of their people, and for the loss of their cove.

"Tell us about the humans," Ninian said. "Tell us how we can defeat them."

"We cannot defeat them in human form," Klaria said. "We're too vulnerable. Our shells are our armour. But we can only defeat them if we all stand up to them. If we all storm the beach together they will be afraid, and they will flee, and then we'll get our cove back."

"Can you lead us?"

Klaria's heart dropped and she shook her head. "My shell is broken beyond repair. I can't help anyone now."

An older woman stepped forward and took hold of Klaria's shell. "You would not still live if your shell was destroyed beyond repair," she said. "There are salves that can help a damaged shell." She turned Klaria's shell over in her hands. "I don't know how much we can help this one, but we can try." She called over several of the younger women who retrieved their shells and, in crab form, disappeared into the sea.

"While Isla seeks to mend your shell, we must make plans," Ninian said. "You must tell us the weapons of the humans."

Klaria nodded and thought of all the things that could be used as weapons. Of what she would use for a weapon, if she needed to. "They have bows and arrows, and spears for hunting fish, and nets to tangle their prey. If they come from their gardens they have forks and spades and hoes and axes. There are rolling pins, and heavy pans."

Anabelle shook her head. "What are all those things? What do you mean?"

Klaria explained in detail, the size and shape and sharpness or bluntness of the item. "Their heavy items could crack shells, but their sharp items may be deflected."

She looked around at the group around her. "They are superstitious. If we gathered the crab-folk from all along the coast and swarmed the beach together we might scare them so that they ran at first sight and we did not have to fight."

The other crab-folk nodded, taking in Klaria's words.

"Then that is what we will do." Ninian turned to face the gathered crowd. "We will wait until Isla returns with her salve, and we will see if Klaria can be healed. And then we will storm our cove, and reclaim our space!"

A cheer went up through the crab-folk.

That night Klaria ate the food of her people; limpets, and seaweed, and tiny shrimp. The salty freshness brought tears to her eyes, as she realised how many years had passed since last she'd eaten food that she truly loved.

They sat on their shells and spoke of the passing years, and their different experiences, and in the early light of dawn Isla and her assistants returned. Isla held a clam shell, shut fast, and passed this to Ninian before she removed her shell.

In human form she turned to Klaria. "I do not know how well this will work. I've never seen a shell so badly burnt, where the wearer was still alive. It may be too far gone."

Klaria closed her eyes as Isla smoothed the salve over the shell first, and then over Klaria's burns.

"Face the moon before it sets completely," Isla instructed, and Klaria did so, aware of the growing light behind her as the dark ahead began to fade.

Her burns tingled, the puckered skin on her face stinging as the salve did its work.

She didn't dare look at her shell.

As the moon dropped below the horizon, Isla massaged Klaria's back. "Shall we try it now?"

Klaria swallowed the lump in her throat, trying to ignore the swirling in her stomach. She held her shell. The top side was still cracked, the softer underside still hard. "Will it work? Would it be better to give it longer?"

"If it does not work now, it will never work."

Klaria nodded, and squeezed her eyes shut tight as Isla lifted the shell and placed it across Klaria's shoulders.

Klaria held her breath.

Across her back she felt the tiny tendrils of the two parts of her body reach out to each other, and connect.

Her eyes flew open. "It's working," she whispered.

But then it stopped.

The shell fused with Klaria's shoulders, but Klaria's body was not pulled inside.

Klaria's heart pounded as she tried to fold herself into her shell, tried to pull the now-hardened underside of the shell around her chest, but nothing took hold. "Argh!" She spun around, screaming her frustration at the sky. "I'm ruined."

She felt a light touch through her shell, and glanced to see Isla examining her.

"You're not ruined," Isla said. "You're merging just isn't complete."

Isla bent down to tear long strands of seaweed from the rocks at their feet, and strapped the now-brittle under-shell together across Klaria's chest. "Let's see," she said, lifting her own shell. "Come into the water with me. Let's see if you can breathe and swim. You might still be able to lead us. You might be stronger than you were before."

Klaria doubted it, but still she followed Isla's crab form into the water, her shell an extra weight on her shoulders, her six crab legs waving about uselessly.

Her heart sank in her chest as the water rose about her, covering her knees, her thighs, her hips. How could she possibly be of any use to anyone like this?

She hoped for nothing more but that the weight of her shell would send her to the bottom, where she could leave the pain of this life behind.

But as the water covered her shoulders Klaria felt lifted by sea. She took a deep breath, closed her eyes, and submerged herself beneath the surface.

Strange grey swirls swam before her eyes, and it took her a moment to work out that she was seeing through her crab eyes. She released the breath in her lungs, only to find her lungs had merged into gills and she could breathe.

Isla's claws clattered together in front of Klaria's face, expressing joy in Klaria's strange new form.

All of a sudden, the clicking noises around her became clear as speech, and Klaria understood that all her people had gathered around to offer support and share their joy that she was with them again.

"We will face the humans tonight," Isla said. "We will storm our cove, and reclaim it for our people."

"I am deformed," Klaria said.

"You are you, and you are back, and together we are all stronger."

Klaria forced a smile, though inside her stomach churned. Her people needed her. They could not continue to live as they were. Perhaps feigning confidence would be enough?

The crab folk gathered in the deep of the cove, and spent the day feasting on clams and snails and algae. Above the waves the afternoon wore on, as below they told stories of the times when they were free to shed their shells and take human-form, and sing and dance in ways they could not under the sea.

As the light filtering through the water faded, the crab-folk began their scuttle over the sea bed, determination bouying their spirits.

By the time they reached the shallows, the moon was visible just above the horizon.

Klaria, Isla, and Ninian approached the surface, their crab-eyes extended above the water.

As Klaria had seen on her first night in the town, fisherman were gathered along the shore, great nets spread out. People walked the shoreline, couples, friendship groups, singles.

Klaria held her breath. Was Pedro there, somewhere? Was he searching for her, or had he returned to their empty mountain home? Did he feel as lost as she had felt, when he first took her shell and hid it away?

All around her the crab's shells clattered together as they tried to settle. Her heart seemed to beat just as loudly. Couldn't the humans hear it?

Klaria saw no indication from those on the shore.

She took a deep breath, exhaling forcefully as though doing so could expel the tiny fish darting about in her stomach, and clicked her claws twice in the sign to charge.

All around her, crabs surged up the beach.

Klaria watched as the humans turned, shouted and stared.

They didn't run.

Why didn't they run?

"Fresh crab tonight fellas!" one fisherman called, gathering one end of his large net. The others followed suit, and soon nets stretched across the length of the beach, several men on each end as they walked back towards the water, scooping up crabs in their wake who ended up upside down and sideways as the nets caught them up and they were tumbled over each other.

"No." Klaria stood, but in the chaos the men paid no attention, and they came around behind and then pulled on the net, scooping up all the crab-folk and dragging them up the shore.

Klaria was face down in the sand, her arms and legs tangled up the net, almost smothered by crab-folk.

That's when the killing started.

Thuds and thwacks from the human's clubs filled the air. The cracks and crunching of shell, and the cries of her people, mingled with the excitement of the humans at such a feast.

"No!" Klaria twisted her head, spitting out sand. "Help."

"Wait," a voice called in the darkness. "There's a woman in there."

"I'll save her."

Men walked across the net, their heavy boots cracking open the shells of those they stepped on.

Klaria's stomach lurched at the sound.

"Stop, please."

The net around her was cut away, the crabs picked up and thrown.

Klaria felt a hand on her own shell, felt it being lifted, then dropped.

"The crab's trying to eat her!"

From the corner of her eye Klaria saw the man lift his club. "No, please."

Down it came, pain shooting down her spine as she screamed out for help.

"We'll get it off you, don't worry."

Another thwack across her shoulders. Klaria bit her tongue, a sharp tang filling her mouth.

"Stop." Klaria's cry was strangled.

"Help me with this, will you?"

Four hands this time, on either edge of her shell.

She was lifted for the briefest time, and then dropped again, her head thumping on the hard sand beneath her.

"What the—"

"What is she?"

This time a hand came under Klaria's shell, and pulled her over onto her back.

Two faces looked at her in disgust.

"She's one of those crab people. From the stories." A young man spoke, his eyes wide.

"Don't be stupid," his companion laughed. "That's just a myth."

"Look at her." An older man stepped into Klaria's view, nudging her shell with his foot. "She's a crab person all right."

The second young man grimaced. "Monster!" he shouted, raising his club in the air.

"Wait!" Another voice, a familiar voice, and as Klaria blinked in a losing battle for her vision, Pedro's face swam into view.

"I'm sorry, love," he said.

Then the world went black.

When Klaria woke, all was quiet.

She was still on the beach, but had been moved up to where the sand was softer. Towards the sea she could see movement, human figures lifting things from the sand and carrying them down to the ocean.

Crabs. Humans were carrying crabs, which hung limply in their arms.

She'd failed.

She'd brought destruction on her people, not salvation. Now they not only had no cove in which to safely change form, their entire community had been slaughtered.

"You're awake."

Klaria glanced up to see Anabelle watching over her. "Anabelle. You're alive?"

Anabelle smiled. "Of course I'm alive. And Ninian, and Isla. They're down there with the others, helping to heal the wounds of the injured."

"The injured?" Klaria frowned and glanced back across the beach.

Now she realised that none of the human figures wore any clothing, that they all carried the crumpled crabs carefully as they carried them to the sea.

To the sea, Klaria realised. Not to their village, to a cooking pot or fire.

These weren't humans, they were crab-folk in human form.

"What happened?" She glanced back at Anabelle.

"You don't remember?"

Klaria shook her head.

"Your husband came. He cried over you. He kept saying he was sorry for having stolen so much of your life, and for the damage he did to your shell. He told the other humans to stop. He said it wasn't worth it, he asked who the real monsters were, those being killed, or those doing the killing. He said they must give us back this cove, that no human must step foot here again. Look." Anabelle pointed up to the hilltops all around, where Klaria could see men, hammering at stakes in the ground.

"They are fencing the area off, so that no humans will come again. You won us the battle, Klaria. You returned to us our cove."

Klaria couldn't believe it. "Is it real?"

Isla approached. "The sea is healing our injuries," she said. "And the humans have left. It's real."

Klaria pushed herself to a sitting position, suddenly aware her shell was no longer attached to her shoulders. "The sea can't heal me," she said.

Isla shook her head. "No. But we can visit you now, as we couldn't before, and you can wear your shell and visit with us under the waves, in your new form."

Klaria swallowed back the lump in her throat. She could not return home, not properly, but she was alive, and she was back with her people.

As the days passed the crab-folk brought driftwood and built Klaria a home on the shoreline. She kept her shell on the wall above the mantle, taking it down whenever she needed to be submerged under the waves, and when the moon was full joined her people in human form to dance and sing and celebrate as they always had.

And the humans kept their word, and the crab-folk never had to fear them again.

About the Author:

Heather Ewings is a Tasmanian author of speculative fiction. With a Masters in History and a fascination with myth and folklore, Heather's stories explore the past and the present (and occasionally the future) through the lens of the magical. Her short stories have been published by Black Hare Press, Asymmetry Fiction and Lite Lit One, and her debut novella 'What the Tide Brings' *was published in April 2020. More information about Heather's writing can be found at* www.heatherewings.com.au.

THIS IS THE DAWNING
(PART VII)

Helena McAuley

By the time I manifest again it is dawn. I'm standing in Pisces'
garden; cool, golden light breaking through morn clouds of heavy-
laden blue-grey, the world awash with serenity.

And I don't know how I got here . . .

My hand is shaking. It grasps at my face, runs trembling fingers
through my hair. Was that real? Did I really do that?

Did I kill Taurus . . ?

I remember anger—rage, even. One moment of thoughtless
fury, and I had cost Taurus his life. The hopeless trembling
consumes me and I fall to my knees. In my mind's eye, I again see
Taurus fall dead into the dirt of a lonely truck stop. Dead by my
hand. Will they have found his body by now? Or will it, too, have

to wait for the rising sun? It was only one incarnation, there will be others. He is not truly dead—none of us can truly *die*. But it is murder, all the same. Not death through combat at the Dawning, not a justified battle of wills.

I killed him where he stood. Without provocation, without giving him a *chance*.

And then . . . What? Unmanifest, I could have returned here in an instant, but I did not. I remember blind rage and all-consuming wrath. But I do not remember where I had been, what I had done—if I had done anything at all.

The trembling subsides, but all it leaves is a vacant astonishment. A deep sense of shock that lives in my chest and the pit of my bowels, immobilising me, rendering me unable to form the thoughts or make the most basic of decisions. I cannot tear my eyes from my hands.

I killed Taurus. My fellow. My brother.

I am no better than Sagittarius.

"Cap? Is that you?" Pisces calls from the doorway. "Capricorn, I didn't realise you were back. What are you doing in the grass? Come inside."

The plan . . . The *order*. It will be forfeit now. They will turn against me for this action and turn their back on what we—*I*—have worked so hard to create.

Resolve steels my gut. No. The *plan* is all there is left. It *will* be achieved, by any means necessary. My actions this night only serve to prove the strength of my will.

"Cap? Are you okay?"

I stand. I speak. "Yes." And my voice holds a strength I did not think myself capable of.

"What were you doing in the middle of the yard?" Pisces asks as I step aside her. "Where have you been all night?"

"It doesn't matter," I tell her. She will not know. None of them will know—cannot know, cannot *fathom*—what I've done.

What I had to do.

What I may yet be *required to* do.

"Where is Douglas?" I ask her. "We have work to do."

"I'm going to emanate and you're going to defend yourself," Capricorn said.

Doug had barely been offered the opportunity to wake up, and with Pisces' 'no caffeine' rule, the struggle was real. "That sounds dirty."

Capricorn's eyes narrowed. "What?"

"Nothing."

Obviously, Cap hadn't woken up on the wrong side of the bed—one needs to actually go to bed for that to occur. For Doug, sleep had been mostly long periods of semi-unconsciousness. There had been moments when he had risen close to waking, hanging in a state of calm, exhausted apathy, and listened to Pisces quietly pottering around the house or OM-ing in blissful meditation. Then he would be claimed, as if between moments, and would fall into the deep, dreamless realm.

Then Capricorn had woken him with one fell shake.

Doug had only managed to rouse himself enough to void his bladder before he was ordered into the backyard, ready to perform this ridiculous experiment.

"How the hell am I supposed to defend myself?" Doug asked, his voice fierce with fatigue. "I'm still human, as you keep reminding me."

Capricorn turned on him. "Instinct." From his hand leapt a beam of yellow light that consumed half of his palm.

With a none-too-manly shout, Doug raised his arms before him. The emanation burnt no worse than the height of the summer sky.

"Good," Capricorn said. "Now let's try one that might actually damage your skin."

Doug blanched. "What?!"

The next emanation was a continuous stream of energy that did not quit until Capricorn desired. The pain as the beam hit Doug's arms was only enough to make him grit his teeth. But it built. A roar escaped him as he fought the desire to pull his burning limbs from the incandescence. He couldn't hold on, the pain was too much; like thrusting his arms onto a burning stove, and masochistically leaving them there.

He swore as he tore his arms from the light, and—to his relief— Capricorn ceased the emanation as Doug broke away. Gasping and shaking, he looked at his forearms; matching red welts covered his skin, not quite blistering.

He whimpered.

"Better," Capricorn acknowledged.

Cap, what are you doing? Pisces' voice entered Doug's mind more easily than it had before, like a wet hand sliding into a glove. Maybe he was starting to get the hang of this.

He needs to know how to protect himself, was Capricorn's response.

The red welts were already dimming to mere pink.

He's human*, Capricorn. He won't be able to defend himself against emanations until he incarnates.*

He's doing alright, so far.

That's because you're not trying very hard.

"Hey," Doug said, "I *can* hear you, you know? But I agree with Pisces. This is stupid."

Capricorn raised an eyebrow at Pisces, who had the decency to look embarrassed. Without turning his head, Capricorn raised one hand.

The emanation caught Doug unprepared, and his shoulder exploded in a ball of fiery pain. Another scorched his leg, causing it to buckle beneath him.

"*Capricorn!*"

Doug looked up in time to see flinty eyes trained on him. "No, wait!"

The next hit his chest, throwing him across the yard and setting his shirt to smoulder. Capricorn advanced on him, burst

after bright yellow burst firing from his palm and striking Doug
with renewed agony.

"Stop!" he cried.

"*Aries* would not stop," Capricorn growled from between
clenched teeth. Doug rolled away in time to save himself from
another volley, which left a ring of blackened grass. "*Sagittarius*
would not stop!" A bolt caught his hand, and Doug retreated with
a yelp. "Any who side with them *will not stop!*"

Doug scrambled backwards in the grass, his leg useless at his
side. His shoulder felt broken, his hand burnt raw, his chest
throbbed as though he'd been run through by the Sword of Uriel.
His back came up against the fence, there was no more ground to
retreat. With cold building horror he looked up at Capricorn and
knew—though he did not know how—that the demigod was no
longer holding back.

Pisces appeared beside Capricorn, bodily grabbing him.

"You'll *kill* him!" she shrieked.

Capricorn threw her across the yard without breaking stride.
"Better me than them." He raised both hands. "Goodbye,
Aquarius."

Doug had no time to do any more than curl his arm across his
face and prepare for burning oblivion. But the pain never came.
All he felt was the mildest sensation of pressure.

Tentatively, he opened his eyes. Capricorn's emanation bore
down on him, splitting and spilling over him, but the world
seemed silent and still. Pisces lay in the grass, her eyes wide and

mouth agape. She wasn't staring at Doug—not quite. Her astonished eyes were fixed *just* in front of him.

It took him a moment to see it. Past the blinding yellow of Capricorn's death ray there was an undertone of soft blue, like the finest, palest glitter imaginable caught in a breeze. A mere sheen against the sky, it curved back on itself, catching and deflecting the emanation like a shield, with Doug cradled inside.

The sensation of pressure increased to a thrust, and Doug's arm began to bow. He pushed back; physically, but also with some other force that he couldn't spare the presence of mind to comprehend. It was like trying to turn away the tide, to push against gravity, or to refute the weight of the sky bearing down on him. He brought both arms to bear and summoned that instinctive might, pushing the emanation from him as if pushing away death itself.

Capricorn broke first, and Doug fell against the fence exhausted.

"Better," Capricorn said. "But there is still room for improvement." He turned away from Doug and stalked towards the house. "Come on. We're going to find Cancer."

Pisces had risen from the grass and intercepted him. "How did you know he could *do* that?" she hissed.

Capricorn threw Doug one solitary glance.

"I didn't."

The bus ride into town was endured in silence. Doug kept his head down, mostly staring at his hands. The scorch marks were gone. He didn't know how, but when he had stripped in Pisces' bathroom, his skin was bare, though the memory of the pain remained.

Now his hands felt as unfamiliar to him as the clothes he had borrowed. He studied the nails, the fine hairs on his knuckles, the intricate pattern of rivulets in the skin. And he stole furtive glances at Capricorn's hands; hands that could bring burning pain. He noted they were larger, smoother, without the discoloured skin and marks normal for a man of his age. But, of course, Capricorn was not a man of his age. He was ageless. The Incarnation of the Constellation of Capricorn. Or of the Zodiac sign? Doug didn't know. Were they one and the same? Or was one a collection of stars and the other a primeval force?

It had certainly *felt* primeval when Capricorn had been trying to assassinate him. Doug let his eyes slip away from those hands and his shoulders hunched further. He remembered the cold look in the older man's eyes as he had assailed him with yellow fire. What was the term they used in *End of Fantasy*? Wrath and Ruin. It had always filled Doug with a sense of supremacy, to rain down Wrath and Ruin upon his digital foes. Now he had experienced it firsthand, and he felt a pang of sympathy for all those poor devastated pixels. But *he* was real, not a computer simulation. And *he* hadn't been attacked in fair combat. *He* had been assaulted by his mentor—a man he'd thought was his friend.

THIS IS THE DAWNING (PART VII)

And yet, his body had responded in kind. Maybe not with killing flame, but with an emanation of his own. The blue shield, sheltering and protecting his frail body. He tried to dredge up the sensation, the force of will and mind that had saved his life. But he couldn't. Even after experiencing it, the power felt as alien to him as a fish trying to breathe air. Like it hadn't been *him* at all.

His eyes strayed back to Capricorn's hands, and then to his own. He understood suddenly why they felt so strange. They weren't *his* hands at all. Not anymore. Now they belonged to Aquarius.

Capricorn pushed the button for the next stop and stood without a word. It took Doug a moment to gather himself so he could follow. The older man alighted the bus and started up the street without even checking to make sure Doug was following. With his taller stance and longer stride, Doug would have to jog to keep up. Part of him thought he should, but instead he simply trudged behind.

Capricorn stopped. "Say it."

"Say what?" Doug mumbled.

There was a twitch to Capricorn's features. "The cogs in your mind turn so loudly I'm surprised your head doesn't rattle," he growled. "Whatever it is, just say it."

Doug looked away. "Nothing."

"Then stop pouting like a petulant child." He turned away.

Doug watched him for a moment, his hands clenching and unclenching by his side.

"You tried to kill me."

He hadn't shouted it, he'd not said it with any real volume, and yet Capricorn still halted in his step, catching the sound on the air. Doug felt his heart beat faster and he wished he could take the words back. He realised he didn't know Capricorn at all.

Capricorn was before him in an instant—dissolved into the air and manifest again right in front of him. Doug flinched and froze, unable to keep his breaths from coming too fast, his muscles rigid and braced for assault. The stern mask of Capricorn's visage melted into confusion, and then alarm. The demigod stalked wordlessly away.

It took Doug a few more moments to calm his racing heart and conjure the presence of mind to follow. Last night he had made a promise to himself that he would support this broken man. But was it possible to do that, and not also become broken?

They left the city streets and entered an alleyway, cobbles under foot and cafés and eateries by their sides, still shut against the morning milieu. From this alley, Capricorn led them down another; smaller, tighter, lined with dirt and crates rather than restaurants. In the back corner of the alley was a door. Capricorn stepped through the artifice of wood and metal and Doug heard locks turning. Capricorn opened the door from the inside and beckoned him to follow.

Beyond the door, a narrow flight of stairs took them into the dark bowels of the building. As Doug's eyes adjusted to the gloom, his ears also began to pick up the sounds of music.

THIS IS THE DAWNING (PART VII)

Nothing you could dance to—not sober, at least—but it was mesmerising, almost soporific. At the foot of the stairs Doug recoiled and swore; there were bodies.

"They're not dead," Capricorn assured him quietly. "They're just . . ." He searched for the right words. "Taking a break from reality."

"What the hell is this place?" Doug hissed.

"Cancer's side project," Capricorn replied. It didn't sound as though he approved.

As they picked their way over the bodies in the narrow hallway, Doug realised it was not just dark, but hazy. A substance that was not quite steam and not quite smoke filled the air with a cloying sweetness and an acrid edge. It clung to the low ceiling in great boughs, hung like bunting. Doug stifled a cough that nearly became a retch.

Capricorn led him to a door that had been torn from its hinges, with a red velvet curtain hung in its place. When the curtain was drawn aside it was breath, as well as smoke, that caught in Doug's throat. Two words immediately came to his mind: 'den' and 'iniquity'.

The hazy air and hypnotic music concealed a chamber of luxurious hedonism. The sultry half-light revealed bodies in stupor, intertwined, or half clad—and sometimes all three at once. Bottles, shisha, and more obnoxious paraphernalia littered tables, chairs, and even the floor. Doug tried to avert his gaze, but there seemed no safe place for it to rest. His neck and ears burned, and more primal, unexpected, urges stirred within him.

And on a raised divan, in the middle of it all, lounged a corset-bound goddess. Beneath it she wore a dress that covered her from neck to ankle, but the demure attire was in opposition of the translucence of the cloth, bound at the wrists by thick leather cuffs, with a slit ran in the skirt from thigh to ankle. Nails and lips painted the colour of blood, she sat proudly; like the Night Queen surveying her kingdom of darkness. Black hair covered her like a shroud, streaks of grey betraying her nature.

Doug swallowed with effort. "Cancer."

"An unfortunate name, in this day and age." The words dripped from her lips like honey, cutting through the noise and gloom without effort. "But one I feel I have embraced." Dark, glittering eyes of deepest brown slid away from the cavorting before her and fell upon Doug. Her smile was bright and brittle as a knife. "I see you approve, Aquarius."

Doug only whimpered.

She beckoned him with one long-fingered hand. "*Come to me.*"

His feet moved of their own volition, without thought or bidding from him. But he was brought short by Capricorn's arm across his chest.

Cancer laughed, a high laugh as brittle as her smile. "What's the matter, Capricorn? Afraid I'll damage him?"

"You can't command him, Cancer," he growled in return.

"Evidently, I can," she rejoined. "He is still *human*, after all."

"He is one of the Twelve, not another of your *playthings*."

The laugh sounded again; as filled with joy as it was consumed with threat. "Dear Capricorn. If you were any more repressed you would be inside out. You should visit me for something more than *business*. I can accommodate any proclivity, and I make no judgements." She beckoned again. "Douglas."

This time Doug was in control of his faculties, and hesitated. He glanced at Capricorn, but the look he received in return was unreadable. How quickly he fell back into old habits, how quickly he placed his faith. Capricorn purported to want to keep him safe, but had attacked and threatened him. Capricorn couldn't expose him to physical danger and then insulate him from something as benign as drugs and sex! Doug was a *man*, after all, not a child.

Unable to keep the indignant expression from his face, he broke away from the man and approached Cancer. She readily drew him into her arms—long, sensual arms, just made for embracing—and he toppled onto the divan. His neck and ears were set to burning again, his vision full of *breasts*.

"You can touch them, if you want," Cancer purred in his ear.

A manic giggle escaped him.

"We're here for your pledge, Cancer," Capricorn admonished her.

"I gave it to Pisces yesterday morning," she dismissed, her eyes not leaving Doug's.

"Pisces says otherwise."

Cancer gave a dramatic sigh and ran the fingers of one hand through Doug's hair. "What are you doing, going around with this stuffy old fool? You should stay here till the Dawning. You'll find it much more"—she flashed the dangerous beauty of her smile—"*pleasurable.*"

The trill of her voice sent a shiver through Doug that reached into places he would rather not think about.

"Cancer," Capricorn pressed.

Her eyes flashed. "I deride you, Capricorn," she hissed at him. "Are you really so insecure and paranoid that you would not take me at my word? Am I not also one of the Twelve?"

"And the most given to duplicity," Capricorn said in cool tones, as immovable as a mountain.

"I have neither seen nor heard from *any* of you for decades, and then all of a sudden you send *Pisces* as your whipping-girl?" She turned her attention back to Doug. "I have given my word, Capricorn. *That* will have to suffice."

"Your word?" Capricorn countered. "You have not told us anything. Perhaps you cannot pledge yourself, because you already have?"

"And to whom would I have done such a thing?"

"Sagittarius."

"Sagittarius' campaign does not rely on bullying and sneering, as yours does," Cancer shot back.

"And how would you know?"

218

Cancer huffed again. She ran her hands down the sides of Doug's ribs, firmly grasping his hips and pulling him closer. " *You* understand, don't you, Aquarius?" she purred. "But if you so desire it, I'll happily pledge myself to you in *private.*"

That was a fantasy that would burn itself into his brain—arousing and terrifying in equal measure. "I have nothing to hide from Capricorn," he stammered. "And you don't have to hide anything from me."

Cancer drew his face closer to hers. "You really are a dear, sweet young man," she breathed, her painted lips brushing his. "To think Aries tried to kill you." And she kissed him.

Her lips were sweet and warm on his mouth, and her hands clung hungrily to his back. More than anything Doug wanted to sink into that kiss, forget about Capricorn, forget about the Dawning, and enjoy every carnal pleasure she was offering. But he couldn't. Something was pressing firmly at the back of his mind, something the kiss was trying to eradicate.

He pushed her away.

"How do you know Aries tried to kill me?" he asked in a hoarse whisper.

Cancer hesitated. "Pisces told me yesterday."

"You said you spoke to her in the morning. We didn't meet Mia until that night."

Not a muscle of her face moved, though her eyes seemed darker for a moment. A cold weight grew in the pit of Doug's stomach.

219

"Cap—!"

He was already moving; unmanifest. But this time Doug thought he could discern the slightest blur . . .

Cancer had unmanifest, also, and Doug fell through the space where she had been and struck the divan head first. He pushed himself up and looked around him. The blurs were real, smudged impressions of images against the hazy light—midnight-blue and yellow. They resolidified around the room, once with Cancer's hand around Capricorn's throat, again with his fist raised as if to strike, another in midair, at the moment her nails tore scores into his cheek.

Capricorn fell to the ground, and Cancer's eyes almost glowed like night.

Her voice seemed to come from everywhere at once. "*Protect me.*"

The bodies in the room broke from their stupor and seethed as one mass. They buried what little of Capricorn could be seen and Doug was caught in the swarm. He tried to keep his head above the sea of skin and sweat. "Cap!" he called and was swallowed by limbs.

The breath was crushed from Doug's lungs. He tried to draw more and was suffocated by flesh. He failed his arms and legs uselessly against the tide of people, the crush of their limbs drawing gouges and welts in their own skin. They were too many to bat away, too all-encompassing to gain ground. Doug was going to drown on land. Drown in sweat, and saliva, and blood.

The edges of his vision dimmed. His fingers curled in on themselves like claws. Fingers that were no longer foreign, hands that—though lost—belonged once more to him.

The instinctual power again surged through him, and the darkness was burnt away by a dazzling blue light. He expected the smell of burnt flesh, but the emanation that exploded from his hands was only hot enough to repel, not scorch. It broke the crush of bodies and he fell to the floor, taking only a moment to regain his breath before he scrambled to his feet.

"Back! Back!" he shouted, waving his enhaloed limbs like torches. "Cap?" he called as he approached the curtain. "You here?"

When there was no reply he hesitated. Capricorn may have unmanifest, or he may still be in physical form, trapped beneath the press of bodies. Just as he resolved to re-enter the fray the two burred spectres shot past him. "Cap!" he cried again, and raced towards the stairs.

The bodies he had mistaken for corpses were on their feet, shuffling towards him as mindless as zombies. Doug hesitated for only a moment, then dashed forward. He twisted and weaved as best he could, but still the limbs reached for him. Clawing hands grasped his pants, his shirt, his shoulders and arms. By the time he was ascending the stairs, he was dragging people behind him like the tail of a macabre comet.

He made it to the top of the stairs by force of will and turned the handle. It was locked. He reached for the bolts, but they were sheered away. There was nothing to grasp. Doug slammed the flat of his hand against the door and whimpered. He summoned the corposant flame, but it had no effect. The weight of the bodies was becoming too difficult to withstand, he was going to topple.

He fell against the door, ready to weep in terror. He was going to die. *Not here!* he pleaded. *Anywhere but here!* It was like the hell of Dante, or the nightmare of Christian Rosenkreutz, swarmed by mindless bodies. His options were slim: to fall and dash himself against the stairs, or be suffocated by walls of flesh.

He summoned the last of his courage and pressed himself as hard as he could against the door. It gave way and he spilled onto his hands and knees in the street. The air had chilled and it was raining now. Doug drank in the cool air and sobbed with relief.

There was a thud from behind him, and with a gasp he turned towards the zombie horde. But the door was shut, still barred from the inside. Doug's mouth fell open.

Had he just *unmanifest?!*

There wasn't time for him to ponder further. The midnight-blue ghost shot through the doorway, followed closely by its yellow twin. Doug watched as they entangled before him like enraged will-o'-the-wisps, then split apart and raced out of the alleyway. A moment later he was on his feet and running after them.

By the time he had made it to the mouth of the alley, the two were manifest again, Capricorn holding the woman down, his teeth bared. Cancer let out a shriek of terror as Capricorn raised his hand in a killing strike.

222

"Capricorn!" Doug screamed. "Don't!"

His call was enough to give them pause, both heads snapping towards him. Cancer's dark, glittering eyes focused on him, brittle and pleading.

"Remember Thálassélas," she said, and was gone; unmanifest from beneath Capricorn, the tendril of pale midnight-blue flashing from the laneway to the city beyond.

Capricorn pushed himself from the ground, visibly shaking with rage.

"What is *wrong* with you?" he roared.

"Me!" Doug cried back. He raced forward and pushed at Capricorn with both hands. "What the hell is wrong with *you*?" He slammed his fists into Capricorn's chest. "Were you just going to let Queen Beryl's zombie freaks drag me to hell?"

"You just added another to Sagittarius' ranks," Capricorn spat.

"Wake up, Cap! She was already there! She was *playing* us! It's because of *me* that you even *know that.* And, what? Were you just going to *kill her*?"

"If she is against us, she threatens the plan."

Rage twisted Doug's stomach. He lashed out at Capricorn, but the blows fell useless against the older man. Doug turned and stomped up the sodden laneway before bellowing a curse to the sky.

"I lived a *boring* life!" he raged at Capricorn. "The worst thing that's ever happened to me was having my wallet stolen at an all-night kebab shop. But since meeting you yesterday I've nearly been killed three times! And one of those times was nearly *by you*! You said to me—you *said* to me! You told me not to leave your side. I thought that meant you were going to *protect me*! Instead you run off to *kill* someone! What *the hell* is *wrong* with you? These people are *your* people, Capricorn! Sagittarius murdered Gemini and it sent you to DEFCON 1! But then you're just doing the *same thing*? *What the hell is wrong with you!?*"

Capricorn's returning gaze was cold.

Rain had soaked Doug's shirt, his hair, was dripping from his nose. It cooled his blood too rapidly, and with it the heat of his ire left him. He sank down into the sodden laneway and shook his head, throwing his hands up helplessly. "Cap," he pleaded. "What happened to you? This isn't the guy who stood in my flat yesterday. Something's happened."

Capricorn looked away. "You're right," he said. "I should have protected you." He squeezed his eyes shut. "It's the *Dawning*." His voice was taut with strain. "You would know if you were incarnate. It's a physical pressure—more than that," he corrected himself. "It's a *spiritual* pressure. I'm sorry." And Doug could tell he truly meant it. "I lost focus. I won't let it happen again."

Doug pressed his lips together. "It's worse for you, isn't it?" he asked. "Because you've been incarnate for so long. That's what Pisces meant."

Capricorn held his gaze. "Yes," he admitted. "But, Douglas, the plan *must* succeed. It's the only thing that matters now. Not me, not any of the Twelve. Only the *plan*. And that means you,

224

too." He approached him and crouched down before him in the rain and mud. Even crouched he towered over Doug. "I need you to understand; none of us will come out of this with clean hands."

Doug let out a long breath. "I'm starting to get that, yeah."

"Are you still with me?"

Doug took, held, and released another breath. "Yeah." He nodded. "Yeah, I'm still with you." He gave Capricorn a stern look. "But you have to be with me, too."

"I am."

It was an impulse, but Doug leant forward and wrapped his arms around Capricorn, squeezing him tightly.

"Douglas," Capricorn said quietly. "Let go of me."

Abashed, he withdrew. "Sorry, Cap."

Capricorn took his hand and drew him from the mud. "What do we do now?" Doug asked.

The older man huffed. "Let's make sure none of our other allies have betrayed us," he said. "Or if, come the Dawning, you and I will have to kill them all."

To be continued in the next edition of the Zodiac Series—

Leo . . .

About the Author:

Helena McAuley has been surviving the covid-19 pandemic by social distancing, not visiting friends, not leaving the house even for exercise, and drinking too much. Actually, in retrospect, covid has not changed her life at all.

When not busy fearing for the state of her liver, Helena uses her technological prowess to fix her aunty's phone, her mum's DVD player, and to get them on 'The Facebook'. She had learnt that it really is best to just turn them off and on again, but it is difficult to reboot family.

'This is the Dawning' is a serialised debut that will be published throughout the ASF Zodiac series. Will Cap and Doug have any allies left to stand with them at the Dawning? Not sure. You'll have to read Leo to find out.

Helena can be found (mostly) twit-ing, (sometimes) insta-ing, and is (rarely) facebookified under the handle @thathmc

Unlike goat-fish, many, many crabs were harmed during the making of this anthology. Not by the authors or editors of the anthology, crabs were just being caught and eaten. There is no correlation.

ABOUT AUSSIE SPECULATIVE FICTION

Aussie Speculative Fiction is a recently established group which was created to support and promote Australian speculative fiction writers.

Check out our links:

www.facebook.com/Aussiespeculativefiction/

www.twitter.com/aussiefiction

www.aussiespeculativefiction.com

www.books2read.com/rl/asf